AF434148

A Little Something Sweet

Laura Ashwood

Anchored Soul Publishing

Anchored Soul Publishing

A Little Something Sweet

Copyright © 2022 by Laura Ashwood, Laura Ashwood Books LLC

All rights reserved. The book contains material protected under International and Federal Copyright Laws and Treaties. No part of this book may be reproduced or transmitted in any form or by any means, electronic or mechanical, including photocopying, recording, or by any information storage system without express written permission from the author.

This book is a work of fiction. The names, characters, places, and incidents are all products of the author's imagination and are not to be construed as real. Any resemblances to persons, organizations, events, or locales are entirely coincidental.

Scripture taken from the New King James Version®. Copyright © 1982 by Thomas Nelson. Used by permission. All rights reserved.

LAURA ASHWOOD

Cover Design by Carpe Librum Book Design.

Get A Free Book!

You're just a moment away from:

* A FREE book

* VIP notice of sales and freebies

* Author happenings

* Great recipes

* Exclusive giveaways

* Special bonus content

* First peek at new covers and titles

Just scan the QR code to sign up for Laura's newsletter, or visit www.lauraashwood.com!

Also by Laura Ashwood

Contemporary

Royally Unexpected

A Little Something Sweet

One Sweet Christmas

Women's Fiction

Summer at Bluefin Bay

Historical

A Groom for Ruby

A Groom for Violet

A Groom By Surprise

Courting Danger

"And be kind to one another,
tenderhearted, forgiving one another,
even as God in Christ forgave you."

~ Ephesians 4:32

Contents

Chapter 1

"**S**PENCER, YOU READY TO go, buddy? We don't want to be late." Jake Sullivan took one last sip of coffee from his mug and grabbed his keys from the hook on the cabinet next to him. It was Spencer's first day back at school after spring break. He had tried to allow a little extra time for his six-year-old son to settle back into his normal school day routine, but it was time to go.

"Dad, I'm already waiting for you," a little voice called from the entryway.

Sure enough, next to the door, his bright blue backpack secured on his small frame and his lunch bag in hand, stood Spencer, shifting his weight impatiently from one foot to the other.

"I didn't think you were ever going to finish your coffee." Spencer frowned at him, his hazel eyes rolling in annoyance.

Jake smiled and tousled his son's blond curls. "Let's go, then."

"Stop it, Dad. You're going to mess up my hair." Spencer brushed Jake's hand off his hair and patted it back in place as they walked to Jake's pickup truck.

Jake raised his eyebrows but didn't say anything as he buckled Spencer into his booster seat behind the passenger seat of the truck. *Since when did Spencer care about his hair?* He pulled out of the driveway, and they drove in silence for a few minutes while Jake thought about his son's sudden change in attitude regarding school. It had been a battle getting him ready in time and back into a routine after the Christmas break. What was different this time? *Cindy.*

Spencer had split his Christmas break between her and Jake. He was always a handful when he returned from time with his mother in California. He was supposed to have gone there for spring break too, but

Cindy had canceled at the last minute. She was an actress and apparently had a chance to audition for what she had said was a *major role*.

Jake understood the lure of fame, but it had been hard to explain to Spencer. He'd been disappointed, but he'd seemed to enjoy the week anyway, spending most of it at Blessed Beginnings, the antique store Jake's parents owned. Jake didn't know who enjoyed the time more, his parents or Spencer.

Spencer loved helping out at the store. He greeted the customers and tried helping them find what they were looking for, and carefully made his own displays with non-breakable items given to him by Jake's mother. But he'd tell you his most important job was making sure everyone took regular cookie breaks. The customers seemed to enjoy his *help* as well.

Jake glanced at his son through the rearview mirror. Was Spencer happy? Was he enough for his son? Emotion pricked the backs of his eyes. Jake had been raised to understand that family came first, no matter what, and he still struggled at times with guilt over his divorce. He'd tried to be happy with Cindy, tried to work through their many differences. Eventually, though, it became apparent that wasn't possible. Their relationship hadn't been based on love, and without that foundation, it hadn't taken long for it to crumble. But he'd gotten Spencer out of it, and Spencer was his pride and joy. The two of them, with a little help from his parents and sister, did just fine by themselves. *Didn't they?*

Spencer had spent most of the week with Jake's parents while Jake finished a job in Helena. He normally didn't take out-of-town work, but because Spencer was supposed to have been in California, he'd accepted the work.

He lifted a small prayer of thanks for his parents and caught Spencer's gaze in the rearview mirror. "I know it wasn't as fun as California would have been, but did you still have a good week?"

Spencer grinned. "Yeah, I love working at Grandma and Grandpa's shop. I even got to help Grandma make the cookies this time."

The kid loved cookies, a trait Jake was certain his young son got from him.

Spencer's smile faded. "I don't really like it in California, anyways. I like staying here better, with you."

His little voice wasn't much above a whisper, but the words hit Jake like a punch to the gut. "I thought you had fun when you visited your mom."

"It's okay, but she always has to talk to people on the phone and see people, and it's kind of boring most of the time. I always have to wait."

Jake pressed his lips together into a thin line. Cindy had always put herself and her needs first. He'd have to have another talk with her about making sure she gave Spencer more quality time when he went for his visit this summer. He had three scheduled trips to see her every year. Cindy had cut their Christmas visit short because of a commercial shoot she'd agreed to do at the last minute. But she was still Spencer's mom, Jake reminded himself. He just wished one day she'd realize what a gift that was.

"She's pretty busy with her acting," Jake agreed. "But I know she loves you and loves spending time with you." He hoped the words sounded more sincere to his son's ears than they did to his own.

"Yeah, I know," Spencer replied quietly.

"You seem pretty excited to get back to school." Jake changed the subject. "You excited to see Josiah again?" Josiah had been Spencer's best friend since preschool. He'd been gone during spring break, visiting his grandparents in Nebraska.

"Yeah, and Allie too."

Allie? Jake couldn't remember hearing about Allie before.

"Who's Allie? Is she in your class?"

"She's new. She's all the way from Florida. She said they have sharks in Florida," Spencer said, his voice filled with wonder.

"Yes, sometimes they do," Jake said. "Are you and Allie friends?"

"She's my girlfriend," he replied, very matter-of-factly.

Girlfriend? Jake snapped his head around to look at his son in the back seat and narrowly missed sideswiping a parked car. He quickly corrected the truck, returning his focus to the road and swallowing hard. Surely he'd heard wrong. *Since when do boys have girl-*

friends at the age of six?

"Your what?" He stole a glance at his son more safely through the rearview mirror this time.

"My *girlfriend,*" Spencer replied and rolled his eyes.

They pulled up in front of Cherry Valley Elementary School, and Jake put the truck in park. He turned to look at Spencer.

"You . . . have a girlfriend?" Jake rubbed the scruff on his chin as he tried to remember how old he was when he had his first girlfriend. *Megan.* He'd been twelve and she'd been his only girlfriend until Cindy. Pushing those unpleasant memories back to the recesses of his mind where they belonged, Jake focused on his son.

"Yeah, and I've been thinking about it, and I think you should get a girlfriend too, Dad," Spencer said, an earnest expression on his young face.

Jake hadn't dated since he and Cindy got divorced. He wasn't about to make another mistake that could potentially hurt his son. He'd already made enough mistakes when it came to women. A girlfriend was the furthest thing from his mind. When had it landed on Spencer's radar?

"I need a girlfriend? I wouldn't know where to find one."

"It's easy." Spencer smiled. "You just tell her she smells nice."

"And that's how you got a girlfriend?"

Spencer nodded, his curls bobbing up and down. "And I told her she is pretty. And smart. Girls like that." He waggled his eyebrows.

Jake suppressed a chuckle as he got out of the truck and went around to let Spencer out. His six-year-old son had more game than he did. He wasn't sure if he should be proud or embarrassed.

"Well, thanks for the tips," he told his son as he unbuckled him and helped him to the ground. "I'll remember that if I meet a nice girl. Have a fun day at school."

"Okay, Dad." Spencer took off at a run towards the front doors of the school and then paused and turned to look over his shoulder at Jake. "Make sure she can make good cookies too, like Grandma does," he called, then ran into the school.

Jake walked into Blessed Beginnings, still bewildered over the discussion he'd had with Spencer. He poured himself a cup of coffee in the large office/break room and grabbed a muffin from the tray on the counter before settling at the table to look over the schedule for the day.

"There you are," Cathy Sullivan said as she entered the room. "How did it go with Spencer this morning?"

Jake looked up from his notes and met his mother's gaze. She wore her usual khaki pants with a flowing floral-print tunic and a pair of black Crocs. Her hair, once blonde but now almost totally grey, was pulled back into a low, short ponytail. Her bright blue eyes sparkled as they always did when she talked about Spencer, and Jake couldn't help but return her smile.

"It was an interesting morning." He took another sip of his coffee and leaned back in his chair, stretching his long denim-clad legs out in front of him.

Cathy, now with her own cup of coffee and muffin, took a seat across from him at the table and raised one eyebrow. "How's that?"

"Apparently, he has a girlfriend."

"Oh, yes. Allie." Cathy nodded and bit into her muffin.

Jake stared at her for a moment. How had she known about this and he hadn't? He pulled his legs in and leaned forward.

"You knew?"

Cathy swallowed her bite of muffin and wiped her mouth with a napkin. "Oh, Jake, I think it's cute," she finally said. "Let him have his fun."

"Since when do they get girlfriends in kindergarten?" He ran his hands through his hair, recalling the rest of his conversation with Spencer. "That's not all." He pinched the bridge of his nose, closed his eyes, and let out a breath before he continued. "He also said I should find a girlfriend too and was actually giving me tips on how to get one."

Cathy's mouth twitched. "Well, he makes a good

point. It's been what, four years since your divorce?"

Jake's brows drew together and he shook his head. *Was this a conspiracy?* "Believe me, this wasn't where I saw myself at my age either—divorced and trying not to mess up my son because of my mistakes. But Spencer and I are fine, just the two of us." He leaned back in his chair again and savagely bit the top of his muffin off. He should have been at the top of his game, and he should have been with Megan. He swallowed the lump of regret that threatened to choke him, along with those thoughts.

Cathy reached across the table and placed her hand on his arm, her expression soft.

"I know you're fine, Jake. And you do a great job with Spencer. I just want to see you happy too."

Jake closed his eyes for a moment before he met her gaze. He knew she meant well; he just knew he was never going there again. His only goal was to be a good dad to Spencer.

"I know, Mom, and I appreciate it, but I *am* happy." He shoved the rest of the muffin into his mouth. "What's on the docket for today?" he asked around the mouthful of food.

Cathy stood and picked up a piece of paper off the desk behind her. She walked back to where Jake sat and gently smacked him on the shoulder.

"Don't talk with your mouth full, son," she gently chided as she handed him a slip of paper. "You'll never get a girlfriend that way." She snickered and tousled his hair.

Jake narrowed his eyes and glared at her for a second before he gave in with an amused grin. He knew how lucky he was to have people around him that cared, even if they annoyed him sometimes. When he moved back to Caribou Falls a few years ago with a toddler in tow, his parents had been instrumental in helping him get settled into life as a single dad. He'd worked for them in the antique store and had taken on refurbishing old furniture. Discovering he had a gift for working with wood, he began taking on remodeling work and eventually started his own business as a historic renovation contractor. He glanced down at the work order in his hand. It was an address on Main Street, not too far from the shop.

"The old Main Street Bakery?" he asked, picturing the empty storefront on the corner of the block.

Cathy nodded and handed him another muffin. "Yes, someone bought it last month and they want to reopen it."

The back of Jake's throat tightened as he recalled the many trips he'd made there with Megan when they'd been younger. She'd always wanted to run the bakery. They'd spent hours talking about the kinds of desserts she'd create there.

Megan was his first love, maybe his only real love, until he'd messed it up. She'd left Caribou Falls while he'd been in California, and he hadn't seen or spoken to her in years. What was she doing now? Was she happy? An image of her smiling face filled his mind, and he stared at the words on the work order until they swam together in a jumble of incoherent letters. He gave himself a mental shake and shifted his gaze back to his mom. No sense dwelling on what he couldn't change.

"That's great," he said. "It's been empty for a long time. I wonder what kind of shape it's in."

Cathy leaned her hip against the desk and grinned at him. "Dad went through it, and it really doesn't need that much work, just a little time and some TLC," she continued. "It should only take a few weeks. Could be a fun project."

Jake raised his brow at her choice of words. *TLC?* He normally did his own scheduling, but occasionally his parents brought in a client or two through their antiques business. This must have been a referral that came in while he'd been in Helena. It was good timing. While Jake's remodeling business was finally getting off the ground, there were still gaps in between projects. This project would fill one of those very nicely.

"I'll head over there as soon as I finish my coffee, thanks."

"That's a fine idea," she replied, her eyes twinkling as she went through the door into the shop.

Jake's gut was telling him something was amiss, but he chalked the feeling up to the unexpected conversation he'd had with Spencer and picked up the muffin while he reviewed the work order again. *A bakery.* Spencer was going to love that.

Chapter 2

MEGAN TURNER SAT INSIDE her car next to her mom and took a deep breath, trying to slow her racing heart. Her gaze shifted between the set of keys lying next to a birthday card in the envelope she held in her shaking hands and the brick building they were parked in front of. A bright red SOLD sign leaned against the dirty window. She gingerly pulled the keys from the envelope and turned them over in her hand.

Is this for real?

"Happy birthday, honey!" Ann Turner leaned across the car's center console and wrapped her arms around her daughter's shoulders in a warm hug.

"I . . . I don't understand," she murmured, staring again at the brick building in front of them. Was she dreaming? She'd pinch herself but was afraid she'd wake up.

Ann Turner lifted her hand to Megan's cheek and gently turned her daughter's head until their eyes met. Her fingers were cold on Megan's cheek, despite the unseasonably warm spring temperature.

"It's yours, Meg. All yours." Ann's eyes shone with pride. "You always dreamed of having your own bakery; now you can. You've given up so much for me. It's time for you to be happy, to live your dream."

Tears filled her eyes and blurred her vision. Megan had always dreamed of owning her own bakery but had abandoned that dream a long time ago, along with another dream she knew would never come true. She wiped her eyes and studied the building that, by way of the keys she held in her hand, was now hers.

The two-story building stood on the corner of the block, situated in such a way that the entrance to the bakery was in the corner of the building. Megan remembered stopping here as a kid when it used to be Main Street Bakery. She and Jake would ride their bikes from the antique store Jake's parents owned to the bakery almost every afternoon and buy cookies. In high school, it became a quick stop on the way to school for a pastry or donut. It closed right before they graduated and had sat empty ever since. Jake had always told her it would be hers someday.

Jake. They'd had so many dreams that would never come true. Because of him, Megan never planned to return to Caribou Falls, but when her mom was diagnosed with breast cancer two months ago, she didn't hesitate. Thankfully, she'd managed to avoid running into him so far.

Megan had left her job as a pastry chef in a posh hotel in Billings and had spent the time since she'd been back in the quaint town, reevaluating her options. While she had loved the creative part of her job at the hotel, her boss had been difficult at best and had continually taken credit for Megan's creations. When her mother got sick, it hadn't been a difficult decision for Megan to leave. She'd also left behind a relationship that had been going nowhere. A true "it's not you, it's me" situation. In this case, it was her.

Since Jake, Megan had had very few relation-ships—if you could even call them that. She hadn't found anyone she really connected with and, if she was being honest with herself, she hadn't really tried. Her stomach twisted and she tried to push those thoughts away as she looked at the keys in her hand again.

Her gaze went back to her mother. "But, how can you afford . . ." The words fell short of a sentence as a sudden realization hit her. *The cancer*. Her mom had told her they'd caught it early and the doctor had given her a very good prognosis, but what if that had changed?

A burst of adrenaline shot through Megan's body, and she grasped her mom's hand, again feeling the coldness in Ann's fingers. Ann wore a pretty coral floral-print scarf around her head and a cream-colored jacket over a coral tracksuit. Her once-short auburn hair was now gone, but she'd refused to wear a wig. She'd said everyone knew she had cancer, anyway; why bother trying to hide it under a scratchy wig?

"Mom, is it . . . the tests . . . are you . . ." Megan choked out the words, unable to finish. Her eyes burned as they welled with tears.

Ann squeezed her daughter's hand and patted it reassuringly.

"No! No, I'm fine," she said.

"Would you tell me?" Megan barely dared to ask the question. Her mom was all she had left. Her father had been killed in a car accident the summer after Megan had graduated from high school. The summer that changed everything. She couldn't bear to lose her mom too.

"Megan, look at me," Ann said softly. It was a technique she'd used since Megan was a small child to ensure her words were being heard.

Megan swiped a single tear from her cheek and did as she was told. Her gaze searched her mom's kind blue eyes for the truth she prayed was the one she wanted to hear.

"I'm fine, okay? Nothing has changed, and yes, I would tell you," Ann said. "The last round of tests actually came back better than they'd hoped." She smiled.

"But then why . . ." Megan cut a glance out the window to the building and then back to her mom.

Ann patted her hand again. "When your father was killed, do you remember that lawsuit that followed?"

Megan shifted uncomfortably in her seat. She didn't like thinking about that period in her life, when everything seemed to have gone pear-shaped. One minute, she and Jake were swimming at Brush Hollow Reservoir, laughing about their plans for the "best summer ever," and the next, she was sitting across the table from her mom, having the rug pulled out from under her life.

"Honey, there's been an accident at your dad's work." Her mother's words echoed through her head. After the funeral, Megan vaguely remembered her mom mentioning bits here and there about meetings with lawyers, but she'd chosen to block most of the memories from that summer.

"Sort of," she replied with a grimace.

"Well, because the accident wasn't your father's

fault, the insurance company filed a lawsuit," Ann explained. "There was a fairly large settlement."

It was coming back to her. Megan recalled having to write a victim impact statement, but she'd never had to go to court and she hadn't thought about it since. Her eyes filled with fresh tears. She'd always been somewhat of a daddy's girl, and his passing left a hole that could never be filled.

"Your father always had big dreams for you," Ann said, her eyes becoming unfocused with the memories. She glanced out the window and then back at Megan. "He'd want this for you, Megan. It's the right time."

"But you need that—"

"Don't you worry about me," Ann interrupted. "There's more than enough left for me. Take this and make your dreams come true. Do it for him, for yourself . . . for me."

Megan wiped at the tears that streamed down her face. So many emotions coursed through her until she couldn't decide if she should sob, laugh, or leap for joy. She reached across and pulled her mom into a tight hug.

"I don't know what to say, Mom. Thank you just doesn't seem like enough," she said through her tears. This time, they were happy tears.

Ann pulled back and wiped a few tears off her own face. "Just make it happen," she said with a grin and glanced at her watch. "I'm sorry we have to go before you can look inside, but I'll be late if we don't leave right now."

Megan's gaze shifted to the clock on her dashboard. Her mom was right. They had just five minutes to get to the hospital for Ann's chemotherapy treatment. She looked back at the building for a moment, her heart and mind full of excitement and ideas, then slipped the bakery keys into her jacket pocket, turned the key in the ignition, and backed onto Main Street.

Megan parked her car in front of Brewed Awakening and patted her jacket pocket as she got out. The jingle of the keys filled her with a sense of purpose and hope she hadn't felt in a long time. Her mother had insisted that Megan go to her new bakery for the few hours the chemotherapy treatment would take, assuring her she'd be just fine with a new book she'd been waiting to read.

Despite her excitement to see the inside of the building, Megan knew the quick stop at the coffee shop was a good decision the second she caught a whiff of the enticing aroma of freshly ground coffee beans. She'd fallen in love with fresh-roasted coffee while she'd lived in Billings and was excited to see that Caribou Falls had acquired a coffee shop since she'd been gone.

The shop was busy for a weekday, and Megan let her mind wander while she waited in line, picturing how she might set up a display case and decorate her bakery. *A name. I need a name.* While the Main Street Bakery had been quaint, she wanted to give the business a fresh look, including a different name. She was so lost in her thoughts, she didn't realize the line had moved forward until a young man stopped next to her and nudged her arm with the corner of the dish bin he gripped with short, stubby fingers.

"Hi, I Lucas," he said and flashed her a wide grin, a sliver of his pink tongue just peeking from between his teeth.

The young man's almond-shaped eyes and button nose made it obvious he had Down's syndrome. She returned his smile.

"Your turn now," he said and trotted off before she could thank him.

She turned to the counter.

The barista greeted her with a friendly smile. "Welcome to Brewed Awakening. How can I help you today?"

Megan stepped forward and noted the name tag on his shirt read Paul.

"Hi, Paul," she replied. "I'll take a large vanilla latte."

"Would you like to add a muffin or apple turnover?"

Megan thought for a moment. It had been a long time since she'd eaten a pastry she hadn't made herself, and it *was* her birthday, after all.

"A turnover sounds delightful." She smiled.

"For here or to go?"

"To go, please." She handed Paul her debit card and tried to be patient while he ran it through the machine. *A bakery. Of my own.* She still couldn't believe it was true. She'd been saving diligently for years to one day buy her own shop, and that money would now come in handy for any renovations and equipment she'd need to purchase.

Slipping her card back into her wallet, Megan stepped aside to wait for her order. Her phone pinged, and she pulled it from her pocket and opened the message from her mom.

ANN: Forgot to tell u carpenter coming to bakery at 11 love u, Mom

Megan placed a hand on her chest, her heart feeling very full. *Can she read minds too?*

MEGAN: You think of everything, thank you Mom <3

ANN: Happy birthday! :D

Megan glanced at her watch. It was now 10:45. Paul reached across the counter and handed her the latte and a small paper bag containing the pastry. She thanked him and ran back to her car, more excited than ever.

The trip to the other end of Main Street took only a few minutes. She slid out of the car and stood on the sidewalk in front of the building for a moment, taking it all in. It felt so surreal. This was *hers* now.

She lifted her gaze heavenward for a moment. *Lord, I'm not sure what I did to deserve this, but thank you.*

The bakery was one of the oldest buildings in downtown Caribou Falls. The brick facade was worn and covered with layers of dirt and grime but looked to be in good condition. Nothing that a little elbow grease wouldn't fix.

Megan slid the key into the lock, turned the brass doorknob, and pushed open the door. The old bell above the door jingled, startling her for a second. Dust motes floated through the sunlight that filtered through the dirty plate glass windows. Stains and grime caked the linoleum floor—which was peeling in some areas. A thick layer of dust also covered the service counter and glass display cases. She walked across the room, the fall of her boots echoing slightly in the empty space and set her pastry bag on the counter. It was perfect.

She spent the next few minutes looking over the space before the contractor showed up. In addition to the sales floor, there was a small office, a walk-in cooler, a small storage room, and a large kitchen. Much of the equipment from the original bakery remained, including ovens, baking racks and two industrial mixers. Megan hoped with a good cleaning, they'd still be in working order. Making a mental list of the other equipment she'd need, she returned to the counter. She'd be able to use her savings account to purchase some new equipment, but she knew she'd need money for supplies, fixtures, signage, and other things.

Her head swam and she glanced once again at her watch. The contractor was due any minute, giving her just enough time to enjoy her pastry and coffee. Megan lifted the paper cup to her lips and closed her eyes as she savored the smooth, creamy coffee. As she lowered the cup, Megan noticed a message printed under the Brewed Awakening logo. It was partially hidden under the cardboard heat sleeve. She eased the sleeve down so she could get a better look. Beautiful cursive letters spelled out, *Love is sweeter the second time around.*

Megan wrinkled her nose. It was an interesting marketing technique and reminded her a little of the messages found inside the fortune cookies at the Giant Panda Cafe, but she didn't agree with the sentiment. Love had left a bitter taste in her mouth, and she wasn't about to give it another chance. Plus, she now had the bakery to fill her time. She slid the sleeve back over the words and dismissed them from her mind.

The bell above the door jingled and Megan jumped, nearly dropping the cup. She lifted her gaze. A familiar pair of blue eyes stared back at her. Her stomach dropped, along with her latte. There was no catching it this time. The cover popped off the cup as it hit the floor, but Megan could barely feel the hot liquid splash against her denim-clad legs.

"Jake?" She gasped. All the memories she'd buried for the past seven years flooded through her mind, and her heart pounded so loud, she was sure he could hear it.

Despite the small size of the town and the fact that their mothers were best friends, it never occurred to her that *he'd* be the contractor her mother would send to do an estimate. From the surprised look on his face, she guessed he hadn't been told who his client was, either.

"What are you doing here?" His voice rose in surprise.

Megan blinked and tried to pull her thoughts together. "I . . . I own this building. What are *you* doing here?"

He held up a clipboard with several pieces of paper attached to it. "I was hired to work on this space."

He wore a pair of faded denim jeans, leather work boots, and a Sherpa-lined denim jacket over a green-and-blue plaid flannel shirt. His dark blond hair was a little longer than the last time she'd seen him, and it curled slightly at the ends. The day-old scruff on his chin only added to his rugged good looks.

Why does he still have to look so good? Megan suppressed a groan. What a disaster.

"Clearly there's been a mistake," she finally said, unable to keep the indignation out of her voice. She pulled a stack of napkins out of the pastry bag and crouched down to try to sop up some of the spilled coffee from her boots and the floor. Her heart felt like it was breaking all over again with him so close. At least if she was looking at the mess she'd made, she wouldn't have to look at him.

"Megan, I didn't . . . the work order . . . doesn't have a name," Jake stammered.

She felt slightly better knowing he was obviously uncomfortable too. *He should be. This is all his fault. He ruined my perfect day.*

His footfalls echoed in the empty space as he approached her. She stood and took a step back, increasing the distance between them. He stopped and stared at her for a long moment but didn't say anything.

"Don't worry about it. I'll find someone else to do an estimate." She swung around and strode toward the kitchen, praying he'd leave. If he had any integrity, he would. Especially considering what he'd done to her.

"I've already been hired," he called after her.

Megan paused at the door to the kitchen.

"I am un-hiring you," she said over her shoulder and stepped through the swinging door, feeling the swoosh of air behind her as it swung shut.

Jake's footsteps grew louder. He was following her. *The nerve!* She could feel her chest tighten. She just wanted him to leave. He'd made it clear a long time ago that she wasn't good enough for him. She didn't want him working on the dream they'd spent so many hours talking about. Her dream. He didn't have a right to be part of it anymore.

The door swung open as he walked behind her into the room. "You can't fire me."

Megan spun to face him, her fists balled at her sides.

"I most certainly can." She narrowed her eyes at him. "You aren't the only contractor in Caribou Falls."

"No, but I'm the best."

She huffed out a breath. "Good to see you haven't

lost any of your arrogance."

"Meg—"

She put her hand up to stop him. She didn't want to fight. They'd been there, done that. "I don't want to see you. Just go, Jake," she said in a soft voice.

"The job's already been paid for, Megan." Jake held the clipboard toward her in his outstretched hand. "Look."

Megan could see the red "Paid in Full" stamp on the upper right corner of the paper, but she didn't reach for it. Her brows furrowed in confusion.

"I don't understand," she muttered. "How . . ." Her eyes snapped to Jake's when realization dawned.

"Our mothers," they chorused in unison.

Chapter 3

J AKE PULLED HIS TRUCK to the curb in front of the elementary school and waited for Spencer. Maybe they were wrong. Would his mom really do that to him? Maybe it was a coincidence that his new client just happened to be the one woman he couldn't face. A lump formed in his throat as he replayed the scene at the bakery in his mind and the shock he'd felt at seeing Megan again.

She was still just as beautiful as she'd been when they were together, and he'd been rendered momentarily speechless when she looked at him over the lip of her coffee cup. Her wavy, deep red hair was longer, now falling just over her shoulders, and he recalled the way her cheeks turned a deep pink when she dropped the cup. Megan still wore very little makeup, but she didn't need to wear any at all. She had a wholesome, natural beauty. Always had.

After the nearly disastrous beginning, they'd managed to come to a somewhat amicable agreement before they left the bakery. He made a list of all the work that needed to be done, and they created a schedule that allowed them each to be there, but at different times so they wouldn't have to run into each other. She handed him a key and gave him a weak smile when she drove off, but he could still see the hurt and pain in her eyes. Pain *he'd* caused.

The chime of a bell brought Jake out of his reverie, and he searched for Spencer's blond curls as kids of all shapes and sizes poured out of the school. He finally spotted him walking next to a young girl with short, dark hair. Jake watched as they stopped and talked for a minute before the little girl turned and ran toward a car parked farther down the sidewalk. She stopped next to the car, turned back toward Spencer, and threw him a kiss before getting inside. Spencer made a big show of catching the kiss and waving back at her before he ran to the truck and climbed inside.

The kid is a natural charmer. Jake chuckled to himself as he got his son buckled safely into his booster seat.

"How was your day, buddy?"

"Great! I got to push Allie on the swings at recess, and Mrs. Higgins let me tell everyone about working at Grandma and Grandpa's shop. Can we go there now?"

A vision of child protective services coming to discuss child labor laws with him momentarily flashed through Jake's mind, but he pushed it aside and pulled the truck away from the curb.

"Why did she have you talk about the shop?"

"We got to tell everyone what we did on break," Spencer explained.

"What did Josiah do?"

"He got to see a spaceship and fighter jets!" Spencer unzipped his backpack and rooted around the bottom. "Look what he brought me."

Jake glanced over his shoulder and saw a model

of an MIG fighter in Spencer's small hand. The jet was situated on a makeshift landing pad that had the logo of an aircraft museum Jake knew was somewhere between Lincoln and Omaha, Nebraska. He remembered going there with his parents and his sister, Julie, when he was about Spencer's age.

"That's really cool!"

"Yeah, we're going to play Top Gun tomorrow with Josiah's jet."

Jake could see Spencer in the rearview mirror, flying the jet around in front of him.

"Guess what else, Dad?"

"What?"

"No, you have to guess," Spencer corrected.

Jake thought for a second. "You get to be Ice Man?"

"No, I get to be Maverick. That's not it, though."

"I give up."

"Allie got to go to Disney World, but she said she was too short to ride Space Mountain. She got to ride tea cups that spinned, though, and she said it made her puke," he said with a giggle. "Do you think we can go to Disney World sometime, Dad?"

A wave of guilt washed over Jake as he thought about Spencer's spring break trip that never happened. He vowed to make it up to his son, maybe even this summer if business was good.

"That would be fun. We should do that," Jake agreed. "Was that Allie you were walking with?"

"Yeah, isn't she pretty?"

"She is."

"Did you decide if you were going to find a girlfriend yet?"

Jake snapped his head to the side and glanced at Spencer, who blinked at him innocently.

"No," he finally replied. "It's not that easy, little man."

"Sure it is," Spencer said. "You just find a pretty girl and get to know her." Spencer turned to look out the window. "Like that one."

Jake followed Spencer's gaze. He saw a young woman helping an older woman into the passenger seat of a car parked in the loading zone in front of the hospital.

Wasn't that Ann Turner?

He strained to get a better look. When the passenger door closed, the driver came into full view, familiar red hair blowing around her shoulders in the breeze. Sure enough, it was Megan. Of all the people Spencer could pick off the street, how did he manage to pick the one woman who wouldn't have him if he were the last man on earth? Not that he could blame her. Jake pressed a little harder on the gas and watched in his mirror as Megan climbed into her car and pulled the door shut. Thankfully, she didn't appear to have noticed them.

"She's really pretty," Spencer went on. "She has red hair like Ariel."

"Ariel?" Jake couldn't place where he'd heard the name. Seeing Megan twice in the same day had left him feeling a bit unsettled. What were they doing at the hospital?

"The Little Mermaid, Dad," he explained with a hint of exasperation in his tone. "I bet she smells nice too."

"I bet she does," Jake agreed.

Back at Blessed Beginnings, Jake got Spencer settled in the break room with a plate of cookies and a coloring book before he went to confront his mom. Cathy had just finished a sale and was tidying up the area by the antique National cash register. Jake did a quick scan around the store to confirm that they were alone. They were. Early spring was usually their slowest season, and his dad used that time to go on buying trips for the store. He was due back the next day from a three-day trip to an estate sale in Wyoming. Cathy grinned at Jake as he approached her.

"Jake, how did it go at the bakery?" she asked, blinking at him innocently. It was the same trick he'd seen Spencer use on him earlier.

She knew. A confusing mixture of gratitude and betrayal filled him as he considered what to say.

"How could you set me up like that?"

"I don't know what you're talking about." Cathy rubbed at an invisible spot on the counter.

"The bakery, Mom. You know exactly what I'm talking about."

"It's the slow season. You needed the business."

She shrugged.

"That girl hates me, Mom."

Cathy looked up at him with a piercing gaze and lifted an eyebrow. "Well, can you blame her? Maybe if you hadn't slept with the first girl who'd have you—"

"Mom, stop." Jake ran his hands through his hair. "We've been through this before. We'd had a fight. *She* broke up with *me*, remember?"

Jake would never forget that night. It was his junior year at Cal State, and he had just been offered a contract with a Major League baseball team. He'd have had to leave college before he was done with his classes, but in his mind, it was a once in a lifetime opportunity. It was a no-brainer that he'd drop out of college and take the contract. He'd immediately called Megan, sure she'd be as happy about it as he was. She'd argued with him about it, though.

She thought he should wait until he graduated so he'd have his degree. *"The offer will still be there,"* she'd tried to tell him. He accused her of not being supportive, and it had gone downhill from there. Her parting words telling him they were through, followed by the click of the phone disconnecting, still resonated in his ears and reverberated off his soul. He'd gone out with his frat buddies that evening for a very uncharacteristic night of drinking and had woken up next to Cindy. He'd sent her packing, riddled with guilt.

His many phone calls to Megan went unanswered. He'd dropped out of school and joined the team. A month later, Cindy returned with a positive pregnancy test.

"You didn't have to marry her, Jake," his mom said, as if she could read his mind.

"Yes, I did," he said, his voice barely above a whisper.

"Megan waited for you. She used to come by the store and visit your dad and me. She even helped us out on occasion during the summers."

"Cindy helped out, too." Jake shot back, hating the desperation in his voice.

"I wouldn't call what Cindy did help," she muttered.

They stood and stared at each other for a long moment.

"Whose side are you on, anyway?"

His mom waved her hand in a dismissive gesture. "It's not about sides, Jake. It's about what's meant to be."

Meant to be. Jake gave a rueful shake of his head. He'd suffered a labral tear in his shoulder his first year in the Majors, and he'd brought Cindy and baby Spencer back to Caribou Falls with him while he healed. Cindy hated the small town. She was a California girl through and through, with nothing but Beverly Hills dreams. Jake hoped having her spend some time at Blessed Beginnings with his mom would help the two of them bond, but Cindy spent most of her days on the phone with her friends back in California, complaining about anything and everything she could think of. Nothing in Montana held her interest, and she couldn't get back to Los Angeles fast enough.

Upon his return to California and his team, Jake's worst fear came true. He no longer had a major league arm. His baseball career was over before it had even really begun. He had a new family to support, with no career and no education. Cindy, now faced with an infant and a husband who would no longer be in the spotlight, decided she was no longer interested in being a wife—or a mother. She left them to pursue a career in acting. The minute the ink dried on the divorce and custody papers, Jake and Spencer moved back to Caribou Falls.

"You should have been more careful with her heart." His mom's words broke through his thoughts, grounding him back in the present. "Megan is a good girl."

Jake pinched the bridge of his nose. He knew that. He *knew* that. There wasn't a day that passed that he didn't regret his actions that long ago night, but he wouldn't change them, because it had given him Spencer.

"She would have taken him, Mom," he said in a low voice.

Cathy frowned. "She would have taken who?"

"Spencer," Jake said, his voice quiet. "Cindy said if I didn't marry her, she would've taken him and made sure I'd never see him again."

She reached forward and laid her hand on his arm. "You never told me that," she said, her voice softening.

"Would it have mattered? I screwed up, but I didn't want to make an even bigger mistake by losing Spencer too."

"I never did like that girl."

"She gave me Spencer."

"Well, I guess even a broken clock is right twice a day." His mom sighed and pulled him into a hug, and Jake clung to her for a long moment before he stepped back.

"Seems to me you have a perfect opportunity here to make amends with Megan," she said.

"She hates me."

"Yes," Cathy agreed, "she probably does, but she'll forgive you. Time has a way of healing those kinds of wounds, you know."

Jake thought about that for a minute. *Could she forgive me?*

"Spencer thinks I should ask her to be my girlfriend," Jake said with a chuckle.

"Smart kid." Cathy smiled.

"Yeah," Jake agreed and paused momentarily before asking, "What's wrong with her mom? I saw her helping Ann into the car at the hospital when I picked Spencer up from school."

She shot him a look of surprise. "Didn't I tell you? I was sure I did."

"Tell me what?"

Ann had been best friends with his mom since he and Megan had been in grade school. His mom talked about Ann quite often, and Jake admittedly tuned most of it out. It was a constant reminder of what he'd thrown away. It was quite possible she'd told him and he just hadn't listened.

"Ann has breast cancer." His mother gave him a sympathetic look. "That's why Megan moved back. To take care of her."

Jake's arms went slack at his sides, and an ache filled his chest. That explained the scarf Ann wore on her head. He'd thought it was just some kind of new fashion. He felt sick to his stomach. Her mom was all Megan had left.

"Is she. . . will she be okay?"

"She's almost done with her treatments and is handling them well. Having Megan here again has been a godsend for her."

Jake knew Megan had been living in Billings, but little else. He'd been surprised when he learned she was back in Caribou Falls, but hadn't thought to ask why. He was too busy trying to avoid her. . . avoid the past. Jake swallowed, his throat suddenly going dry. She'd been dealing with this all alone. Again. Just like when her dad died. He'd gone off to college in California and left her behind then, too. Never mind that she'd insisted. He should have been there for her. Then and now. A realization struck him.

"The bakery. . ." he began, but the words wouldn't come.

"Yes, Ann bought it for her so she'd have something." Cathy's expression turned somber. Tears filled her eyes and threatened to spill down her cheeks. "In. . . in case her treatments fail."

"Will they?" His breath caught in his throat at the thought. "Fail?"

"The doctors said they caught it early." She swiped

at a rogue tear as she struggled to regain her composure. "They're optimistic. We're all praying for her."

Jake nodded and thought about what his mom said about Megan forgiving him. *Forgiveness.* It was too late to mend their relationship, but if there was a chance she'd forgive him, maybe they could be friends again. How wonderful would that feel, to have Megan's forgiveness? He wasn't sure how he'd go about it, but he knew he had to try.

Chapter 4

M EGAN WAS QUIET ON the way home from the hospital. She'd sat fuming in the car while she waited for her mom to get wheeled to the patient loading area. It had been the perfect birthday—until Jake showed up. Until they realized their mothers had set them up. She didn't want to seem ungrateful, because she *was* grateful, but she didn't appreciate having them meddle with her personal affairs. Not when it came to Jake.

Megan's mood fluctuated between being giddy with joy to feeling like she was acting like a petulant child, leaving her unsure of what to say. Her mom had been so generous. Incredibly generous, really. But seeing Jake again had stirred up feelings she thought were long gone, and she didn't like it. Feelings equaled pain, and Megan had had enough of that in her life. She didn't want any more, didn't need any more. Her stomach twisted into a knot.

"You're awfully quiet." Her mom's words pulled Megan from her thoughts. Her mom continued. "I'd expected you to be chattering nonstop about your plans. What's going on?"

"Like you don't know." The words sounded awful as they left her mouth, but she was unable to stop them. "Did you think sticking us in the same room would have us falling into each other's arms again?"

Her mother shrugged and lifted her hands in a helpless gesture. "That's how it used to be. We kind of hoped . . ." She trailed off.

She and Jake had been right. It was a conspiracy. Megan should have known she couldn't be in Caribou Falls very long before her mom and Cathy would start meddling with her life. They'd seen how devastated she'd been after Jake had . . . she couldn't even finish the thought.

Megan steered the car into the driveway of her mom's house and slid the shifter into park. She turned and looked at her mom. Ann's face was pale and pinched with exhaustion, but there was an underlying expression of hope. The knot in Megan's stomach tightened.

"It's not that way anymore, Mom," she said, her tone softening a bit. "Now we can't even be in the same room together."

"Why not?" Ann asked.

Why not? Maybe because looking at him tore her heart into pieces all over again. Maybe because it had taken her years before she thought she was over him, only to find out in the span of thirty seconds that she wasn't and probably never would be. Her nose began to tingle, and the steering wheel blurred as her eyes filled with tears.

"Because it hurts," she cried. "It hurts so much, Mom." Tears spilled over her eyelids and fell like rain down her cheeks. "He wasn't supposed to find someone else. We were supposed to be together always. And then . . . and then I lost him, Mom. I lost him, my dreams, my—" A sob choked off her words. She took a shaky breath and continued. "H-he married her and they had a child. And they live in *our* house." Megan dropped her head onto the steering wheel. She could feel her mom's cold hand through the sleeve of her jacket.

"It was never your house, Megan. Don't be so melodramatic."

Megan snapped up her head. Was her mom taking Jake's side? She sniffed and swiped at her cheeks with her fingers. "It was supposed to be," she said, not caring how ridiculous she sounded. "We picked it out senior year. We were going to remodel it. But he did it with her instead." Fresh tears tracked her cheeks.

"You're wrong there," her mom said. "Jake's *ex*-wife never stepped foot in that house. You two need to bury the hatchet and move on." She pulled a tissue from her purse and handed it to Megan. "Now, wipe your eyes."

Megan did as she was told. Even though her mom was right—it had never really been her house—Megan had to admit she felt slightly better knowing that Jake hadn't shared the beautiful Victorian home with his ex. But as far as burying the hatchet? She wasn't so sure about that. The pain still cut too deep.

"Now let's go inside before the neighbors start to wonder what we're doing in the driveway. I need to lie down for a while," her mother said and opened her car door.

A spring breeze came through the open door and cooled Megan's flushed cheeks. She noted, for the first time since she'd picked her mom up, the paleness of her face and the tiredness in her eyes. The back of Megan's throat grew tight, and she gave herself a mental kick. She was supposed to be helping her mom, not whining about Jake. They got out of the car, and she helped her mom into the house.

"Go settle in on the sofa, Mom. I'll make us some tea, okay?"

Her mom squeezed her hand and shuffled toward the living room, and Megan headed into the kitchen to put some water in the electric tea kettle. After selecting a box of lavender chamomile herbal tea for her mom and lemon ginger for herself, she readied two mugs and tried to clear her mind while the water heated. A few minutes later, she stepped into the living room and handed one of the mugs to her mom before she ensconced herself in the plush tan chair which sat adjacent to the matching sofa where her mom was propped against the cushions. A fluffy teal throw lay across her thin frame.

"Are you comfortable, Mom?" Megan asked.

Her mom nodded, then frowned. "Aren't you happy with your gift? You said you always wanted to own your own bakery, and I just thought . . ."

Megan could hear the need for approval in her mom's voice, and a tsunami of guilt and shame washed over her. Her mom had been through so much since Megan's dad died. They'd been the perfect couple, at least in Megan's eyes. Even as a child, Megan recognized the deep love they'd had for one another. Her mom slipped into a deep depression the summer after the funeral, and Megan made the choice to stay behind in order to help her through it when Jake left for college in California.

Once her mom improved, Megan enrolled in the culinary school in Kalispell. Only an hour away, it allowed her to live at home while she attended the school and keep an eye on her mother. She'd planned to join Jake in California when she finished school, but by the time she graduated, he'd gotten married and had a baby on the way. She'd moved to Billings instead, not wanting the daily reminders of her life with Jake in Caribou Falls.

Guilt continued to plague Megan as she thought about how she intentionally avoided coming back to Caribou Falls after she found out Jake moved back. She couldn't face him. But her actions had forced her mom to drive all the way to Billings to visit her only child. Her only family. She'd been so selfish.

Then the cancer came. Her mom had a double mastectomy right away and was now nearly finished with her chemotherapy treatments. They'd been through so much together and had become very close. Her mom deserved far more for her generosity and love than to have Megan do nothing but whine about her hiring Jake. *I'm a terrible daughter.*

Megan slipped off the chair and knelt on the floor next to the sofa. She stared into her mom's pale blue eyes—eyes that were the exact color of her own—and took her hand. Megan could feel the trails of tears as they made their way down her cheeks. *I've really messed this up.*

"Like it? Mom, I love it. I'm still in shock, I think." Megan tried to smile. "What you did, what you've done, is so . . . unbelievable. I'm so sorry if I sounded ungrateful. I didn't mean to . . . I just . . . seeing Jake in person just really threw me off. I love the bakery. Thank you doesn't even begin to cover it, Mom."

"I didn't mean to hurt you." Her mom brushed a strand of hair off Megan's forehead. "Cathy and I just thought with you staying in town and him being in town that maybe . . . it's been such a long time, and you guys were so close once. Plus, he does such a good job with that renovation stuff. But if you want me to hire someone else, I will," her mom said. "I'm sure Jake would understand."

The knife Megan felt in her stomach twisted as she realized the truth in her mom's words. It was time to move on and let go of the past.

"No, Mom. You're right. I'm sure Jake will do a good job. We'll make it work."

Her mom squeezed her hand, and Megan relaxed a bit as she saw relief wash over her tired face. She slid back against the pillows and took a sip of tea, then handed her mug back to Megan. "It sure would be nice if you two could become friends again," she murmured as her eyes drifted shut.

Friends. Could she go back to being just friends with Jake? The man could still make the bottom of her stomach drop without even trying. Was being friends possible? Megan gazed at her mom's sleeping form. The soft sound of her rhythmic breathing as she slept sent a sense of peace through Megan. She didn't know how to be friends with Jake anymore, but she could try. For her mom, she could try.

Megan parked her car in the alley behind the bakery and began unloading the bags of cleaning and baking supplies. After her mom had fallen asleep, Megan was too keyed up to relax, so she changed into an old pair of jeans and a T-shirt and decided to go to the bakery to start cleaning and testing the baking equipment.

She let herself in the back door and placed the bags on the floor in the kitchen, then looked around, still trying to comprehend that this space was hers. There was so much work that needed to be done, and Megan wasn't sure where to begin. *Can I do this?*

The reality of the situation sank in, and fear and self-doubt filled her mind. Megan's eyes began to glaze over and her pulse quickened. She struggled to catch her breath as one of her father's favorite sayings came to her. *How do you eat an elephant? One piece at a time.* One step at a time. Her breathing slowed, and a feeling of calm determination replaced the fear. She *could* do this.

With a notebook and pen in hand, Megan returned to the storefront. Using the sales counter as a desk, she began making lists of what needed to be done. There was a list of things to be cleaned and another of things to be tested. Then she'd start working on a list of supplies that needed to be purchased. When they were in high school, Jake teased her relentlessly about her lists. She let out a long sigh. That seemed like a lifetime ago.

From the corner of her eye, she spied the empty coffee cup from earlier that day and recalled the message she'd seen on it. She picked it up and turned it over in her hands thoughtfully before she placed it on the counter and returned to her lists. After she cleaned and tested all the equipment in the kitchen, she'd start yet another list of what needed to be replaced or upgraded.

Megan straightened and stepped into the center of the room and glanced around, trying to picture how it would look when she finished. A rush of energy and excitement filled her veins and, even though it was late in the afternoon, she wanted to get started on her cleaning list.

Pulling her phone out of her pocket, Megan opened her music app and selected her favorite playlist of upbeat songs. She pressed play, and music filled the empty space, making it feel more alive. She turned the volume up, laid the phone on the counter, and went to work.

"Megan?" a muffled voice called from the storefront a short time later. Megan could barely hear it over her music. "You here?" the voice called again.

Megan wiped her hands and pressed the screen on her phone to stop the music. The only person that knew she was there right now was her mom, and she was pretty sure that wasn't her mom. She pushed open the swinging door and was horrified when it struck someone on the other side.

"Ouch!"

Megan slipped through the doorway. Relief washed over her when she recognized the person on the other side. She made a mental note to lock the door behind her next time she was there alone.

"What are you doing here, Lacey? Trying to give me a heart attack?"

"What are you doing? Trying to maim me?" her best friend shot back.

The women eyed each other for a moment, then burst into laughter and wrapped their arms around each other for a brief hug. She and Lacey Philips had been best friends since Lacey's family moved to town when the girls were in grade school.

"Seriously, what are you doing? Wait, you knew, didn't you?" Megan raised an eyebrow and narrowed her eyes. She was unable to stop the smile that tugged on her lips.

"I might have," Lacey admitted. A smug look crossed her face. "I'm so excited for you!" She hopped up and down and clapped her hands. Her dark blonde hair was pulled up into a messy bun, and she wore stained denim overalls with what was once a red shirt underneath. Lacey was a mechanic at her stepdad's auto repair shop.

"It's still just so . . . surreal," Megan said, looking around the storefront.

Lacey looked around the room and settled her gaze back on Megan. "There's a lot of work to do, that's for sure. But you're going to rock this." She grinned. "And I can help after school, too."

"Oh my gosh." Megan's eyes widened. "Guess who Mom hired to do the remodeling?"

Lacey's cheeks turned pink, and she studied the glass display case at the sales counter. "Just needs a little elbow grease," she said, rubbing at the dust with her fingertips.

"You knew about that too?" Megan asked quietly, her shoulders slumping. *How could my best friend not tell me about something that important?*

Lacey took Megan's hands in hers, her eyes pleading for understanding. "I'm sorry, Meg," she said. "I wanted to tell you, but your mom swore me to secrecy."

"But . . . why?" Megan pulled her hands back and looked away. She felt her throat tighten. "You know how I feel about him."

Lacey took a deep breath and put her hands on her hips. "Because I agreed with her."

Megan's gaze shot to Lacey's, and her mouth fell open. No words came.

"You're going to stay in Caribou Falls now," Lacey said. "You can't avoid him forever."

"I *could* have if you guys hadn't gone behind my back." Megan stared at her for a long moment, then looked away.

"Meg, it's been what? Seven years now?"

Megan nodded but refused to look at her friend. *First my mom, then my best friend.* She felt betrayed.

"You guys were so close."

"Yeah, until he cheated on me," Megan spat.

"He didn't cheat on you," Lacey countered. Frustration filled her voice. "You broke up with him, remember?"

"Whatever." Megan waved her hand dismissively. "It's in the past."

"Exactly. So don't you think it's time you left it there?"

Megan threw her friend a dirty look. "You sound just like my mom."

"She's a smart lady." Lacey's lips curled into a smile. She pulled a small purple gift bag out of the giant purse she carried. "Here," she said, holding it out in front of her. "Stop being mad and open your birthday gift."

Megan threw another glare in her friend's direction before the corners of her mouth lifted in a smile.

She'd never been able to stay mad at Lacey for long. Her shoulders relaxed and the tension evaporated from her body. "I'm not mad," she said, reaching for the small bag. "I just wish I would have known before he showed up."

"You've already seen him?"

"Yes, he was here earlier." Megan pulled the lavender tissue paper from the bag and unfolded it.

Lacey reached forward and stopped Megan with her hand. "Hold on!" she exclaimed. "I want details."

Megan rolled her eyes. "There's nothing to tell. We went through what needs to be done and agreed on a work schedule." She didn't plan to spend any more time with Jake than she had to.

"He still looks really good, doesn't he?" Lacey smirked.

Megan's face flushed, and she rolled her eyes. "He looks the same as he always has."

"Yeah," Lacey said with a chuckle. "Hot."

"Stop already." Megan smiled and batted Lacey's hand away. There wasn't any use denying that Jake was still as handsome as he'd always been. Heat flooded her cheeks, and she dipped her head and focused on unfolding the tissue paper, grateful for the distraction. Nestled inside was a gold cupcake charm attached to a fine gold chain. *It's beautiful.*

"It's not much—" Lacey began, but Megan cut her off with a hug.

"Thank you. I love it. It's perfect." Megan knew her friend was on a tight budget, making the gesture even more special. She picked up the fine chain and carefully fastened it behind her neck, the charm falling just below the hollow of her throat.

"It looks great." Lacey smiled and glanced at her watch. "I'm supposed to meet Brian in an hour for dinner and still need to shower and change. Give me a tour before I go."

Brian was Lacey's latest boyfriend. She had a history of dating a guy just long enough for it to get serious before she found some reason to break it off. Megan gave it another month, two tops. Not that she was one to talk—at least Lacey dated. She gave herself a mental shake and took her friend's arm. She gave her a tour of the space and by the time she was done, she was even more excited than ever about it.

Lacey gave her another hug before she left, with promises to connect over the weekend. Megan walked back into the kitchen feeling very blessed and went back to cleaning. While she scrubbed, her mind kept returning to the words her mom and Lacey had spoken about letting the past go. Could she forgive Jake and move forward with her life? Did she want to?

Chapter 5

JAKE SAT ON HIS sofa and idly flipped through channels on the television. Nothing drew his attention. He glanced at his watch—just after 8:30. Spencer was already asleep after an exciting first day back at school and to Jake, the house seemed even quieter than usual in the darkness.

Since running into Megan earlier, he'd been unable to get her off his mind. He scrubbed a hand over his face and let himself fall back onto the sofa. Jake's gaze wandered the room, and he imagined what it would be like to have Megan there with him, like they'd planned. He closed his eyes for a moment and shook his head. What a mess he'd made of his life.

Feeling restless, he stood and paced back and forth in his living room, his mind wandering to the work that needed to be done at the bakery. It was still early. If his mom would come and keep an ear out for Spencer, he could get a jump start on the work and surprise Megan.

He pulled his phone from his pocket and hit a number on the speed dial. His mom answered on the second ring.

A few minutes later, he heard a soft knock and his mom stepped through the front door.

"Everything okay, Jake?" she asked, a look of concern on her face. "You sounded distressed when you called."

"It's fine. I just thought I'd get started on the work at the bakery."

"Tonight? That's why you want me to stay with Spencer?" Cathy stared at him, eyes wide, brows raised.

Jake looked away and rubbed the back of his neck. "Well, I thought with Dad still gone, you wouldn't mind staying . . ." He trailed off. *Maybe this wasn't such a good idea.*

They stood quietly for a moment.

"You want to go there now so you don't have to worry about seeing her," Cathy said, breaking the silence as she gave him a look of understanding.

Her. Megan. "She doesn't want to see me. We agreed on a schedule, but I thought I could get a jump start on the work while I could. I want to make it easier for her," Jake explained. "And to be honest, I'm a little keyed up from seeing her today. Maybe if I get the work done sooner . . ."

Cathy nodded and slipped out of her jacket. "I think that's a fine idea." She pulled a paperback romance novel out of her large purse and held it up.

Jake couldn't quite catch the title but recognized the cover from when he'd seen the book in the back room at Blessed Beginnings. His mom loved books, a love Jake was grateful she passed on to Spencer.

"I was going to catch up on my reading tonight. I can do that here, too." She smiled.

Relief flooded through Jake. "Thanks, Mom. You're the best." He grabbed his jacket off a hook by the door. "You know where the blankets are, and I'll be back in time to get Spencer ready for school."

He might not be able to fix what he'd done to Megan in the past, but he *could* help make one of her dreams come true now.

Jake pulled his truck up in front of the bakery and cut the engine. The lights inside the building were on. He glanced at the clock on his dashboard—9:00 p.m. Cathy had to drive past the bakery to get to Jake's house, and she hadn't mentioned anything about seeing the lights on. *Was this another setup?* Jake quickly dismissed that thought from his mind; she had no way of knowing he'd be working during the night.

When he'd been there earlier in the day, he'd stayed for a while after Megan had left, making a list of what needed to be repaired and what supplies he thought he'd need. He was sure he'd turned the lights off when he left. *Hadn't I?* There didn't appear to be any movement inside the building. Had she come back and left the lights on? Maybe. Either way, he was glad he decided to work this evening because he could make sure no one was inside, and if he was the culprit, Megan wouldn't know. He didn't need more reasons for her to be angry with him.

Jake slid out of his truck, went around to the back, and grabbed his tools. A crowbar lay along the side of his truck bed and at the last minute, he grabbed that too. Caribou Falls didn't have a high crime rate, but you couldn't be too careful these days. Jake slid his key into the locked door and eased it open so the bell wouldn't chime.

Music blared from the kitchen area. His grip tightened on the crowbar when a voice began singing along with the chorus of the song. A voice he recognized. *Megan.*

Jake stood by the door for a long moment while he tried to decide what he should do. On one hand, he knew Megan was upset around him. On the other hand, his mom was already at his house, watching Spencer for the night. It wouldn't make sense to lose so many hours of work time. He was still contemplating his options when Megan burst through the swinging door that separated the dining room from the kitchen. She stopped mid-bop and a little scream escaped her lips before she covered them with her hands, her eyes wide.

Guess I'm staying. Jake let the door close behind him and set his toolbox and crowbar on the floor. He lifted his hands in a calming gesture.

"It's just me. I didn't know you were here."

Megan slid one hand down and patted her chest over her heart while pointing the index finger of her other hand at him. Her cheeks appeared flushed, but Jake couldn't tell if it was from being frightened or from whatever it was she'd been doing in the kitchen.

"You just about gave me a heart attack, Jake Sullivan. What are you doing here?" She moved her hands down to her hips and glared at him.

She wore scuffed white sneakers and a faded pair of jeans that were ripped at the knee. Jake was pretty sure the hole in her jeans came from being worn rather than a fashion statement. Her untucked grey T-shirt sported purple and gold letters that spelled out Caribou Falls Pirates, with a caricature of a pirate beneath the lettering. Streaks of dirt covered her clothes and arms. She'd pulled up her auburn hair and tied it with a bandana. She reminded Jake of those old posters of Rosie the Riveter. He couldn't stop the smile that played across his lips.

"I didn't think you'd be here," Jake repeated and gestured to his toolbox on the floor beside him. "I thought I'd get a jump start on the work."

Megan glanced at the toolbox before her gaze returned to his. She chewed on her lip—a habit Jake remembered her doing when she was nervous. They stared at each other for a long moment.

"What are you doing here?" he asked, breaking the silence.

"Same," she finally replied with a shrug.

Jake raised his brows and smirked as she glanced down at her clothes and swiped at some of the dirt and dust that streaked them. She then raised her hand to the blue paisley bandana covering her hair, and the spots on her cheeks grew even redder.

"I wasn't expecting to see anyone. You're not supposed to be here . . . the schedule," she stammered.

"I know, but you aren't either," he gently reminded her. "It's all right. I can leave." Jake bent and picked up his toolbox. A heavy feeling spread through his chest; he'd blown it with her again. Resolving to stick to the schedule they'd made going forward, Jake turned and put his hand on the doorknob. "I'm sorry I scared you." He glanced at her over his shoulder and pushed the door open.

"Jake . . . wait," Megan called from behind him.

He paused, the doorknob still in his hand. His name sounded so good coming from her lips.

"You're here, so you might as well work," she said. "I'm in the kitchen. You can work out here."

"Deal." Jake grinned and pulled the door shut and placed his tools back on the floor. The notes of a new song filtered into the room from the kitchen. Jake recognized its catchy beat and smiled tentatively at Megan. "You gonna sing to this one too?" he teased.

A flush crept back into her cheeks. "Don't push it, buddy. You stay in your part of the shop, and I'll stay in mine." Her voice was stern, but Jake could see the twinkle in her eyes and the slightest hint of a smirk on her pouty, pink lips.

He lifted his hands in an "I give up" gesture.

"All right, then." Megan nodded once, as if sealing their deal. "I'll finish cleaning the mixers," she said, but she didn't move.

She stared at him for a long moment, her light blue eyes piercing his soul. Even covered in dirt and grime, she was the most gorgeous woman he'd ever seen. Cindy was beautiful too, but in a different way. She was always perfectly made up and immaculately dressed. The first time Jake had seen her without makeup, he barely recognized her. Megan didn't need any of that. She was naturally beautiful.

And still standing there.

"Go then." Jake jerked his chin toward the kitchen. If she stayed out here much longer, he'd end up saying, or worse yet, doing something foolish, he just knew it.

Megan's eyes widened and she tilted her head back in a defiant gesture. "Fine, I'm going."

"Fine. Go," he retorted with a grin.

They gazed at each other for a few seconds before Megan flashed him the smallest hint of a smile, turned on her heel, and disappeared into the kitchen. Jake stared at the swinging door for a minute. He hadn't realized how much he missed talking with her and how they used to banter back and forth until now. It was one of the reasons she'd stolen his heart and kept it all through high school. Maybe longer, if he were being honest. He let out a long sigh and returned his focus to the job he'd been hired to do.

Jake surveyed the room, trying to decide where to start. The building was one of Caribou Falls' oldest, having survived both the flood of 1964 and the earthquake in 1975. It had started out as a bank and was turned into a bakery sometime in the 1950s when the Nelsons purchased it after a merger closed the bank. It, along with most of the buildings in the four-block radius, was on the National Register of Historic Places. Jake had done several renovation projects in the historic district and was familiar with the regulations on historical preservation set forth by the Historic Preservation Commission.

He had inspected the exterior brick facade of the building earlier in the day and was pleased to note no signs of efflorescence or erosion. The interior walls were also brick and just needed a good cleaning. A stiff-bristled broom with an extension handle would make quick work of that.

Jake studied the linoleum floor for a moment. It had definitely seen better days. Grabbing the crowbar, he walked to the corner farthest from the front door and crouched down. Using the flat edge of the tool, he pried up the corner of the vinyl flooring and carefully pulled it back. His pulse quickened at what he saw underneath, and he rushed into the kitchen to get Megan.

Megan didn't hear his footsteps over the loud music pumping from the phone propped on the stainless steel counter that ran along one wall. Jake glanced around the kitchen, astonished to see the progress she'd made. The stainless steel shelf under the freshly oiled butcher block bread table gleamed. The floor in the kitchen—which had been updated at some point with seamless urethane flooring—had been scrubbed clean. The island's stainless steel surface shone brightly from the center of the kitchen. An assortment of whisks, rolling pins, and other utensils covered its surface.

Megan scrubbed the inside of one of the Vulcan ovens along the back wall, still oblivious to his presence. He tried not to notice the way her jeans hugged her curves as she moved her hips to the music while she cleaned. He cleared his throat and grimaced when she jumped.

"Sorry," he said, gesturing toward her phone. "The music. . . ."

"What's up?" She tucked a stray hair back into her bandana and waited expectantly.

"Come." He beckoned with his finger. "You've got to see what I found."

Megan followed him into the other room and over to the corner. He reached down and pulled back the faded linoleum, exposing beautiful maple flooring beneath. A soft gasp escaped her lips as she crouched next to him and ran her fingers along the surface of the wood. She was so close, their shoulders brushed against one another. Jake could smell the faint aroma of the same musky, earthy perfume she'd worn since high school. Her nearness caused his heart to race, and a shiver of awareness dashed over his skin.

"It's gorgeous!" Megan exclaimed. She looked at him, her blue eyes bright and her smile wide.

Jake's heart beat as erratically as the rhythm of the music that wafted into the room from the kitchen. He forced himself to look away.

"Is it usable?" she asked.

"I'm not sure yet. I just found it." He offered a quick shrug and said, "I'll remove the rest of the linoleum and see what it looks like. If the rest of it is in as good of shape as this section, then yes. I'll just need to sand and refinish it; it will be much cheaper than replacing this vinyl. And because it's not in the kitchen, you don't have to worry about it being an issue with the health department."

Megan grasped the loose edge of the linoleum from Jake's grip and began pulling. "Let's find out!"

"Whoa!" Jake reached out and grabbed her arm to stop her from pulling away the flooring. A shock of electricity went up his arm and traveled straight to his stomach. He pulled his hand away. Her eyes met his. Had she felt it too?

"I need to use a scraper so we don't damage the wood underneath," he explained, returning his focus to the job at hand.

"Oh," she said. Disappointment laced her voice. "I was sort of hoping you could check now. That's okay, though. It can wait. It's not like it's going anywhere."

"I have a scraper in the back of my truck. Let me get it." He smiled. He'd run all the way to Missoula to buy one if he didn't already have one, just to see her smile again.

Three hours later, Jake once again called Megan from the kitchen and stood next to her as she surveyed his work. A pile of linoleum pieces lay in the middle of the room, the entire wood floor revealed. It was in nearly pristine condition. She pressed her hands to her cheeks and tears welled in her eyes. Jake's chest tightened and he rubbed his chin. *Hadn't she wanted it to be usable?*

"Meg? Are you ok?" he asked, uncertain what else

to say.

She nodded and turned to face him. "I'm just . . . gobsmacked." She gently shook her head, her eyes closing for a moment before meeting his gaze again. "I can't believe this is happening to me." Her hands dropped to her sides.

"The flooring?"

She gestured toward the pile of linoleum with one hand. "The flooring." She used the other hand to gesture toward the glass display case. "The bakery." Then she lifted both hands and raised her shoulders. "Everything."

Relief flooded through Jake. He fought the urge to pull her into his arms. "You deserve this," he murmured and found he meant it too.

Chapter 6

T HE EDGE OF THE horizon glowed with bright hues of purple and pink when Megan and Jake decided they were too exhausted to continue. Jake followed her outside, and she could feel him watching her as she slid the key into the door to lock it. Unable to stifle a yawn, she covered her mouth and turned toward Jake. He looked as tired as she felt. Main Street was still and quiet, covered with a light coating of frost that sparkled in the first rays of sunlight. The snow-capped Mission Mountains loomed in the distance.

"I can't believe how much we got done." She sighed, her breath forming little wisps of clouds in the cold air. *We*. She never thought she'd see the day where "we" meant her and Jake, but she found they had fallen into an easy rhythm of working together.

"Yeah, we make a good team," Jake agreed, then seemed to hesitate. A furrow formed between his brows, and Megan noticed a pink flush appear on his cheeks.

"I mean in there . . . the work," he stammered.

We did make a good team, Megan thought. They always had. Like peas and carrots, their moms used to say. But that was a long time ago. Megan felt too tired to think about it—about anything, really—so she just nodded in agreement. They stood in awkward silence for a long moment.

"I think I can have everything done in a few weeks," Jake finally said. "The roll-off will be delivered sometime late this morning. I plan on coming back this afternoon after I drop Spencer off with Mom when he's done with school, if that still works." He rolled his shoulders and looked at her expectantly.

Megan knit her brows together, confused for a second, then she remembered the schedule they'd made. Being accustomed to rising early, Megan had taken the early morning hours through lunch, leaving Jake with the rest of the afternoon and evening. She slowly shook her head. It made no sense at all; why had she suggested that arrangement? Why had he agreed to it? Insisting they use a schedule had been a foolish idea and, at this point, completely unnecessary.

"It doesn't work?" Jake frowned.

"No," she said wearily. "It doesn't." She toyed with a lock of hair. She hated admitting when she was wrong. Especially to Jake.

Jake scrubbed his fingers down his face, rested them behind his neck, and rolled his head from side to side before letting his hand fall to his hip. "All right, you can call me when you leave and—"

Megan shook her head and lifted a hand to stop him. "No, it's the schedule. The schedule doesn't work."

Jake looked at her with a blank expression.

"I forgot about Spencer. You need to be with him after school and in the evenings."

"It's just for a few weeks. I'm sure my folks—"

"Jake, stop." Megan interrupted. "Just bring him with you later. And forget the schedule. We don't need it."

He slid her a guarded look. "Are you sure?"

"About the schedule or Spencer?"

"Both. He's six, you know. He has a lot of energy."

Was she sure? About the schedule, yes. She hadn't known Spencer was six, but she figured he was young. How much trouble could he be? She'd always liked kids. She even taught Sunday school when she was in high school. The kitchen was at a point where she planned to start test baking to get a feel for the ovens. And besides, it was just for one day. She gave Jake an easy smile.

"Yes, I'm sure. He can help me make cookies."

Jake chuckled. "You may regret that offer. He is a cookie fiend."

"Then we'll get along just fine."

Megan surveyed the items spread out on the worktable. She wasn't sure what kind of cookies Spencer liked, but she had a couple recipes she wanted to test, so she figured she had him covered. While she waited, Megan worked on her list of possible names for the bakery. Her mom had suggested simply leaving it as The Main Street Bakery, but Megan wanted it to be different. Something more modern and fun. So far, she hadn't been able to come up with anything that sounded right.

The bell above the front door announced the arrival of Jake and Spencer. Her mouth went dry, and she blew out a series of short breaths. *God, please don't let this be a mistake.*

Taking a deep breath, Megan smoothed the front of her red-and-blue paisley tunic and pasted a smile on her face just as a small boy burst into the room. He stopped in the middle of the kitchen and looked around, his gaze finally settling on her. Megan drew in a sharp breath. He looked exactly like Jake had when she'd met him all those years ago at Bible camp. Spencer's eyes were hazel, where Jake's were blue, but other than that, the resemblance was striking.

"Whoa!" Spencer exclaimed, his eyes wide with wonder. "This is a huge kitchen!"

Jake stepped through the door and raised a hand in greeting. He wore a navy baseball hat with the Sullivan Construction logo stitched above the visor, a few blond curls escaping along the sides. A dark grey T-shirt covered his broad shoulders and was tucked into a pair of jeans. A hint of stubble sprinkled his strong jaw. He stepped behind his son, resting his large hands on Spencer's small shoulders.

"Spence, this is Megan," Jake said, a smile tugging at the corner of his mouth.

The young boy's eyes grew wide, and he tilted his head back to look at Jake. He then turned and tapped Jake's side with his small fingers until Jake crouched next to him. Spencer slid Megan a curious glance and brought his hand up to his mouth.

"She's the one, Dad," he whispered loud enough for Megan to hear. "She's the one I showed you on the street, remember?"

Jake cringed and Megan watched his cheeks flush pink. She was unable to hear his response, but Spencer must have because he turned back to face her and gave her a crooked smile. Light blond curls framed his cherubic face, and his smile revealed a single dimple on his left cheek. Megan couldn't recall having ever seen a cuter kid.

"Hi, Spencer, your dad tells me you like cookies."

The boy nodded vigorously.

"Well, it just so happens that I need to bake some today and thought you might be able to help me out."

Spencer's eyes grew wide, and he turned to Jake. "Can I, Dad?"

Jake nodded. "Yes. Just be sure you listen to Megan and don't get in her way."

Spencer threw his arms around Jake's legs for a brief moment before he stepped back. "Thanks, Dad. I promise!"

Megan watched their exchange and felt a tug on her heart. She'd never given much thought to having a child of her own. When she and Jake would talk about their future, it had always been implied that a family would be part of that future, but she hadn't entertained those kinds of thoughts for a long time.

Seeing the pure love pass between Jake and Spencer created a yearning in her for the same kind of love. If only . . .

"All right, I'm going to work in the other room. Be good," Jake told Spencer, snapping Megan's attention to the present.

"We'll be just fine, won't we, Spencer?" She glanced down and smiled at the child. He gave her a shy smile in return.

Jake tousled the boy's hair and looked at her, his gaze holding hers for a long moment. Megan felt her skin begin to flush, and she looked away. Why did he still affect her this way?

"Let me know if he's any trouble," Jake said.

Megan nodded a response and watched him turn and walk through the doorway. She couldn't help but notice how the snug T-shirt made his shoulders look wider somehow. Giving herself a mental shake, Megan redirected her focus to Spencer.

"Well, Spencer, what should we make?"

Spencer's eyes sparkled with excitement, and he grinned. "Something sweet."

After a bit of discussion, they decided on chocolate chip cookies. They were Spencer's favorite. Megan brought a sturdy chair from the office and set it next to the counter for him to stand on.

They got busy measuring sugar and butter into the mixing bowl. Spencer grabbed an egg from the carton, and Megan watched in awe as the small child carefully cracked it into a measuring cup.

"You've done this before," she exclaimed.

"Grandma lets me help her. We love to bake." He took another egg out of the carton and carefully cracked it into the cup. "You have to add them one at a time," he instructed.

Megan suppressed a chuckle. "I just might have to hire you."

"Really?" He grinned up at her. "Grandma says I'm a good helper."

"She's right."

They spent the next few minutes adding the remaining ingredients and mixing the dough. Megan helped Spencer scoop the dough onto the pans, and then she placed them in the oven and set the timer.

While the cookies baked, she and Spencer gathered some garbage out of the office. He chatted about school and helping his grandparents at the antique store. Megan was surprised to find she was thoroughly enjoying herself. He was a charming child.

Minutes later, the timer buzzed. Spencer climbed back onto the stool and watched as Megan pulled the cookies from the oven and transferred them to a cooling rack. The intoxicating aroma of warm, buttery vanilla and chocolate filled the room.

"Can I test one?" Spencer asked, his eyes gleaming. "Grandma says I'm the best tester."

How could she say no to that face? "Of course you can," she replied and placed a warm cookie in front of him. "Let it cool for just a minute while I run this trash out to the dumpster. I'll be right back."

"Okay, I'll wait until you come back in, but hurry. It smells so good. I don't know if my fingers will listen very long."

Megan suppressed a giggle as she took the garbage out the back door of the kitchen. The boy was adorable. Once in the alley, she walked to where a large, dirty blue dumpster hugged the brick exterior of her bakery. Her bakery. That had a nice ring to it. She smiled and heaved the bag over the lip. Megan turned to go back inside when she heard a rustling sound. She paused and listened closely. There it was again. Something was inside the dumpster.

She rushed over and grasped the lip of the metal container with her hands and tried to peer over the top. Her five-foot-three-inch frame wasn't tall enough to allow her to see more than what was on the very top of the nearly full dumpster. She tried using the toes of her shoes to give herself a boost, but they kept slipping down the smooth metal side of the container. The rustling noise sounded again, this time accompanied by a small mewling sound. It was an animal! Megan let go of the lip and ran back into the bakery.

"Jake!" she called as she ran through the kitchen and burst into the main room where Jake was now sweeping the remaining debris off the hardwood floors.

His head snapped up and his eyebrows drew together in a serious gaze as their eyes met.

"I need your help! Come quick!" Megan beckoned with her fingers.

Jake let the broom fall from his hands, concern morphing into action as he ran across the room. "Spencer!"

"No, Jake." Megan held up her hand to stop him. She hadn't meant to send him into a panic. "Not Spencer, he's fine. It's something outside." She could hear the sigh of relief behind her as Jake followed her through the kitchen toward the door that led to the alley.

"Stay right there, Spence. We'll be right back," Jake called to his son before he stepped into the alley behind her.

"It's in there." She gestured to the dumpster with her hand. "I can't get high enough to see."

Jake stood there a moment, his arms at his sides, his eyes narrowed. "What's in there?"

Megan lifted her hands, palms up, and shrugged her shoulders. "I don't know. I think it might be a baby animal."

Jake's brows lifted and his mouth twitched. "Oh,

Waffles, did you find another baby raccoon?"

A flash of heat spread across Megan's face and the back of her neck at the mention of the old nickname he'd given her. Waffles had been her favorite breakfast food as a child. She and Jake would meet early in the day to hang out together. He'd tease her about smelling like waffles, and eventually started calling her by that name.

One day, when they'd been about ten, they'd ridden their bicycles to Hanging Horn Park—one of their favorite hangouts. Megan had found a baby raccoon under one of the benches in the large log amphitheater. She was certain it had been abandoned, and she'd created such a fuss when Jake wanted to leave it that he ended up riding his bicycle home by himself to get their parents. They called a game warden to explain to her that it was not abandoned so she would leave the small animal.

Megan's gaze met Jake's. How long had he been looking at her? She knew she'd heard something. She chewed her lip. She'd probably die of embarrassment if it turned out to actually be a raccoon. She heard the mewling sound again.

"Did you hear that?" She gestured toward the dumpster in frustration. "Jake, you have to help me find it." She pleaded with him with her eyes. She didn't know what was in there, but even if it was a raccoon, it didn't belong there and would die without their help.

Jake walked to the dumpster and peered over the edge. Megan held her hands to her mouth and watched, barely daring to breathe.

"Well, what do we have here?" he said softly and reached in with one of his long arms.

Megan held her breath as he pulled out a small, dark ball of fur and held it toward her. She looked at it closely. It wasn't a raccoon. It was a tiny, dirty kitten.

Chapter 7

"GRANDMA! GRANDMA!" SPENCER BURST into Jake's parents' house and ran toward the kitchen, not even bothering to remove his shoes. Jake shook his head and bent to remove his boots before he joined them. His mom had invited them over for supper, and Jake had gratefully accepted. While he could manage well enough, he wasn't much of a cook, and he rarely turned down an invitation to feast on one of his mom's home-cooked meals.

"Dad and Megan found a little tiny kitten in the garbage!" Spencer said to his grandma when Jake entered the room. He used his hands to show her his approximation of just how tiny the kitten was.

Cathy cut a curious glance Jake's way before turning back to the boy.

"They did? In the garbage?"

"Yes! Someone throwed it away and Megan put it in a box. We gave it some cream." Spencer climbed onto a stool at the counter and shrugged out of his jacket, letting it fall to the floor behind him.

Normally, Jake wouldn't tolerate that kind of laziness from him, but he decided to let it slide today. He flashed his mom a grin. It felt good to see his son so excited.

"And then Megan put her scarf in the box," Spencer continued. "She might have to throw it away, though, because it got dirty too."

"Throw the kitten away again?" Cathy frowned.

"No, Grandma." Spencer sighed. "Her scarf. She said she was going to give the kitten a bath and keep him, but she let me give him a name!"

"What did you name him?"

"Patches. I wish we could keep him. He's so cute." He shot Jake a wistful look.

"We talked about this, Spencer," Jake said. "That

kitten is too small for me to care for properly."

Spencer's shoulders slumped and the corners of his small mouth turned down. "Everything deserves to be loved. That's what Megan said."

A heavy shot of guilt hit Jake in the gut, but he forced it aside. He wasn't bending on this. He didn't have the time—or the skill—to care for the small animal.

"She's absolutely right," he agreed and tousled the hair on the top of Spencer's head. "And she is going to take great care of Patches."

"What else did you do, Spencer? Your dad said you were going to help Megan bake." Cathy threw Jake a conspiratorial wink. She was great at diverting Spencer's attention.

Jake felt a warmth spread through his chest. He was truly blessed to have the love and support of his parents. An image of Cindy popped into his head. Some people weren't as lucky.

"We made chocolate chip cookies. I even got to add the eggs. All by myself." Spencer grinned proudly. "I wanted to eat them all, but Megan only let me have two." He stuck his bottom lip out in a pout for just a second before lifting his gaze to meet Cathy's. "We even used a super secret ingredient," he said. "They make the cookies taste the best ever!"

"A secret ingredient?" Cathy's brows shot up with interest.

"I can't tell you, Grandma. She said it was a secret, and we can't tell secrets."

"No, I don't suppose we can, can we?" Cathy sighed and leaned forward, resting her elbows on the counter as she scrubbed at a non-existent spot with a kitchen towel.

Jake suppressed a grin. His mom had always taken great pride in making the best cookies of all the moms in their friend group. Learning that Megan's cookies were deemed "the best ever" by her grandson wasn't something she cared to hear, even if it was true.

Spencer was right, however. They *were* the best chocolate chip cookies Jake had ever tasted. Crisp on the outside and buttery gooey on the inside, with just the right amount of chocolate. His mouth watered just thinking about them.

"They are pretty good cookies." Jake grinned, unable to resist the jab.

His mom straightened and waved the towel at him. "That's enough talk about cookies."

Jake lifted his hands in an "I surrender" gesture and laughed.

"Megan is really pretty." Spencer slid a sideways glance at Jake.

"Oh, is she now?" Cathy grinned.

"Yes." He bobbed his head. "Like a princess. *And* she smells good too." He turned and looked at Jake. "I think you should tell her that, Dad. Girls like that."

Jake cleared his throat and tried to think of an adequate, fatherly response, but he came up with nothing. The kid was right, but he couldn't tell her she smelled good, even if he wanted to.

"Things are going well at the bakery, then?" His mom studied him.

Heat crept up Jake's neck and across his cheeks. He lifted his shoulder in a half-shrug. "Better than I thought it would," he muttered.

Her mouth curved into a knowing smile, and Jake

could see the mischief in her eyes. "Mmm hmm." She nodded, then turned her attention to Spencer. "What should we have for supper? Your grandpa is going to be starving when he gets home."

Jake removed a slow cooker full of barbecued meatballs from the trunk of his dad's car and used his elbow to close the lid. Roger and Cathy walked just ahead of him, their arms laden with baked goods. Spencer had spotted his friend, Josiah, as they pulled into the nearly full parking lot and had already run inside the church to find him. Jake dropped the meatballs off on the table that was laden with potluck goodies, and surveyed the crowd.

Grace Church's annual Spring Festival was well under way. Tissue paper flowers hung from the ceiling in the fellowship hall and adorned the many tables that had been set up for the potluck luncheon. In one corner, Spencer and Josiah stood within a long line of children waiting by a table to have their faces painted. Casseroles and desserts of every variety imaginable lined the table before him, and Jake's stomach rumbled in anticipation of all the food. He loved potlucks.

He scanned the crowd for his sister, Julie, who had promised to drive down from Kalispell for the event. Julie was five years younger than Jake. She worked up there as a legal assistant. He hadn't seen her since Christmas and looked forward to spending the day with her.

"Hey, Sully," a familiar voice called from behind him. Jake turned and spotted his best friend, Shane Wickham, walking toward him. Shane was tall, with broad shoulders and short, dark, almost black hair. His eyes were dark and serious, and he'd grown a mustache and goatee since the last time Jake had seen him. They clasped hands and pulled into a shoulder hug.

"Shane, I'm surprised to see you here," Jake said. "You're supposed to be in New York, aren't you?" Shane was a cyber security analyst and traveled all over the country to investigate and prevent cyber security breaches.

Shane shrugged his shoulders and tipped his head

from side to side. "Yeah, I flew in to see Angie and my folks."

"How's that going?"

Shane shrugged. "Same old, same old."

Jake frowned. Angie was Shane's on-again, off-again girlfriend, and judging from the expression on Shane's face, it was off-again. They'd been in that cycle since high school and Jake couldn't figure out why Shane kept going back to her. She was a nice enough girl, but she had a wandering eye—not unlike Cindy.

"I'm sorry, man. You deserve better."

Shane clamped his lips and nodded but didn't reply. His gaze cut into the crowd of parishioners. He spotted his friend Paul Anderson, who waved at him and crossed the room to join them. Paul had moved to Caribou Falls during their sophomore year of high school, but he'd become fast friends with Jake and Shane. He was easily the tallest man in the room and was still trying to fill out his lanky frame.

"Hey, isn't that Megan?" Paul pointed toward the potluck table where Megan was arranging a covered casserole dish.

She wore a knee-length light blue dress adorned with tiny white flowers, and strappy white shoes. Her hair was curled, and it hung in soft waves over her shoulders. She looked so beautiful, she almost took Jake's breath away. As if she felt his eyes on her, she looked up and met his gaze. Her eyes brightened with recognition, and the corner of her mouth turned up in a half-smile. She lifted her hand and gave a little wave before she turned back to assist Ann.

"What's going on there?" Shane asked, nudging Jake in the side with his elbow.

Jake's face grew warm. "Nothing. I was hired to do some work for her. That's all."

His eyes followed her as she gently led her mother to a table and helped her get settled. Her friend, Lacey, was already at the table, and he watched as the three of them visited. Several people stopped by their table to say hello, and Megan chatted easily with all of them. She had such a natural way of making people feel at ease around her.

"Huh. Isn't it strange spending time with her? I

mean after . . ." Paul asked.

Was it strange? Maybe a little, but it felt more like time hadn't passed. He was so comfortable around Megan. He felt like he could be himself around her. She hadn't been at the bakery the last few days, and he found himself missing her presence. He needed to get a grip. It was over between them, thanks to him.

Jake returned his attention to his friends. "What's strange is everyone making a big deal about it." He frowned. "She's a client, a friend."

Shane lifted his hands in mock defeat and grinned. "I hope you don't look at all your friends and clients like that."

"Shut up," Jake said good-naturedly. Shane knew him too well. He heard a high-pitched squeal behind him and turned just in time to catch his little sister as she threw herself at him.

"Jules!" He returned her hug and lowered her to the floor with a grin. Jake towered over his sister, who barely stood five feet tall. Her straight blonde hair fell just to her shoulders and a fringe of bangs brushed the top of her tortoiseshell cat-eye glasses. She wore jeans with a pair of black Chuck Taylor high tops and a black silk blouse. She was a walking contradiction, but somehow managed to make it work for her.

"How's my favorite brother?" Julie beamed.

"I'm your only brother."

"That's why you're my favorite." Julie's gaze traveled to Shane and Paul, and her smile faltered.

"Julie," Shane nodded.

"Hey, Smalls," Paul teased.

He'd taken to calling her that shortly after he and Jake had watched the movie *The Sandlot*. She hated it. Jake noticed a crimson flush creep up her face. At least, she used to hate it. Interesting.

"Hey, Paul," she said, a flush creeping into her cheeks, and looked away. She turned back to Jake. "Where's Spencer?"

Jake's gaze swept the room for Spencer's blond curls. He spotted him just as Spencer wrapped his arms around Megan's legs. He watched Megan stoop down to return his son's hug. An ache filled him deep inside. His grandfather's words came to him. *You reap what you sow.*

Julie followed Jake's stare and her eyes widened. "Isn't that Megan?"

Jake was saved from having to reply by the sound of Pastor Richard clapping his hands to quiet the room. After thanking everyone for coming, he instructed them to bow their heads in prayer. Jake listened intently as the Pastor spoke about spring being a time for new beginnings. How through the miracle of God's forgiveness, we are all given a new beginning, but in order to receive that forgiveness, we must first ask for it. He then blessed the food that was prepared by the loving hands of the congregation and ended with the words, "In Jesus' name, Amen. Let's eat!"

Paul and Shane went to find their families, and Jake went through the line and filled his plate with a variety of casseroles, salads, and desserts. He'd seen Spencer going through the line ahead of him with Megan and scanned the tables until he spotted them. Julie, Spencer, and Megan were on one side of the table and his parents, Lacey, and Megan's mom, Ann, were on the other. Megan waved him over and Jake slid into the empty chair next to Megan.

Megan wiped her mouth with a napkin and smiled at him. "Hey, Jake. I was surprised to see you. I didn't think you'd be here today."

"And miss this?" He gestured to his full plate. "Are you kidding?"

"Jake." Lacey lifted her chin in his direction and smiled. "Good to see you again."

"Hi, Lacey. Back at you."

They ate and engaged in lively conversation as the group caught up with one another's lives. Jake watched Megan easily visit with everyone at the table. They were all entertained as Spencer regaled them with a detailed account of how he won a four-layer chocolate cake in the cake walk. Jake pushed his plate away and couldn't remember ever feeling fuller or happier.

After everyone ate their fill, Julie took Spencer to get his cake. Ann and Cathy went to look at the plant sale, and his dad visited with Pastor Richard, leaving only Jake, Lacey, and Megan at the table.

"I've just about got the floor in the storefront done," Jake said. "I really think you're going to like it."

"I can't wait to see it," Lacey said. "Megan told me it was going to look amazing."

"It really does," Megan said. "Jake's doing a fabulous job."

Her pretty mouth curved into a smile and her gaze held his for a moment before she turned back to her friend. It was the kind of smile that used to melt his heart. Warmth spread through his body.

Lacey cleared her throat and pushed her chair back. "I think I'll go see if I can get another piece of that dessert."

"You didn't have dessert," Megan pointed out.

"Oh, right," Lacey replied, rising to her feet. She twirled her finger next to her temple. "Lack of sugar's making me crazy. I'm going to get dessert, that's what I meant. Talk to you later." She winked at Megan and moved toward the food table.

Megan shook her head, and she and Jake both laughed. They sat in silence for a moment as Jake pondered what to say. He wasn't sure if her absence at the bakery the past few days was because of him or something else. Did he really want to know? Did it matter? He tore at a napkin on the table in front of him. He felt like an awkward, geeky teen all over again.

"You have a busy week, too?" he finally asked.

Megan set down the paper cup of punch she held and nodded her head. "I baked some cakes for the cake walk, but I did that at Mom's house. She wanted to help, but I think she was intimidated by some of the equipment at the bakery."

"Spencer's cake?"

Megan smiled and shrugged. "Maybe. I think we're the only ones that made layer cakes."

"How's your mom doing? I didn't know about the . . . that she was sick. I'm sorry."

Megan swallowed and blinked several times before answering. "She's doing well. She just finished her treatments and has a PET scan in a couple weeks. We'll know for sure then."

"I hope it goes well."

"Thanks, Jake."

They fell silent for a moment, then Jake said, "I

haven't seen you at the bakery for a couple of days."

"Yeah, I had to fill out paperwork at the bank for a loan, then took a trip to Billings to order some equipment from the restaurant supply company there. I probably could have ordered it online, but I wanted to actually look at the equipment before buying it." She sighed. "I think I've taken care of just about everything. Except for the name."

"You don't want to call it Main Street Bakery?"

"If I can't come up with something soon, I'm going to have to." She let out a weary laugh.

Spencer ran to the table with Julie on his heels. She carried a cardboard tray with a chocolate-frosted layer cake that had been carefully covered in plastic wrap.

"What do you have there?" Jake asked.

"That's my cake I won," Spencer gushed, but his expression quickly turned sour. "Auntie Julie said we have to wait until later to eat it."

Julie set the cake on the table next to Jake. "I told him it was too big to eat right now," she said.

"She's right. We can have it later," Jake said. "Maybe we can take it to Grandma and Grandpa's and share it after supper."

"But they're here now. We can share it here," Spencer argued.

"It's a lovely cake," Megan said. "I bet it's chocolate fudge flavored." She gave Jake a conspiratorial wink.

He waggled his eyebrows at her in return. "Sounds like a great dessert for later."

"But I want a treat now, Dad," Spencer whined. "Josiah got to have some of his cake that he won."

"I tell you what," Jake began, hoping for a compromise. "There's a whole table full of desserts over there. How about we get you a little something now, and we save the cake for later. Does that work?"

Spencer let out a dramatic sigh as he stood on his toes to get a better look at the sweets on the table across the room. "I suppose. Are there cookies and those bars with the marshmallows inside?"

"I bet there are. What kind of treat do you want?" Jake asked.

Spencer held his hands up with his index fingers spaced a couple of inches apart. "I just want a little something sweet." He giggled as he moved his fingers farther and farther apart.

Megan's face lit up like someone had just given her a present, and she pulled Spencer into a hug.

"That's the second time I've heard you say that, Spencer," she said.

"Say what?"

"Something sweet. You're a genius. It's perfect! A little something sweet."

Spencer grinned broadly. "I'm a genius?"

Jake's brows dipped. He wasn't connecting the dots. Then all at once it hit him. She was right. It was perfect.

"Yes you are, buddy."

Chapter 8

T HE NEXT COUPLE OF weeks passed quickly. Megan spent the early morning hours making sure her mom was taken care of and settled for the day before she would leave to work at the bakery. While she was done with treatments, the fatigue lingered. The doctors assured them that was normal and her energy levels would pick back up soon. They waited anxiously for the results of the PET scan, but her doctors continued to be optimistic.

Her mom spent a large part of the day sleeping, and Patches—now clean and healthy—had become a good companion for her. Megan knew her mom was almost as excited about the bakery as she was. She agreed to help Megan once it opened, and Megan was excited to work with her. They'd always been close, but it was different now that Megan wasn't a child in school. They'd become friends, too.

She and Jake had fallen into an effortless routine at the bakery. He made it so easy to slide back into their old friendship. He was usually there by the time she arrived, and she'd work in the kitchen or her office while he worked around her. Spencer visited a couple afternoons each week and "helped" Megan test recipes. She adored the child and found herself looking forward to the days he came to help. If anyone would have asked her a month ago if she'd be comfortable spending time with Jake Sullivan, Megan would have laughed. Now, she eagerly anticipated the days they worked together.

Jake had sanded and refinished the maple flooring in the front room and was working on the walls and fixtures. The plumber and electrician had signed off on the plumbing and wiring. Supplies and ingredients were being delivered daily. She'd been taking samples to most of the restaurants in the area and had managed to secure several accounts. The signage was due to arrive the following week, and Megan made plans to hold a grand opening in two weeks. She'd interviewed and hired two part-time baking assistants. The bakery was really taking shape.

She had just pulled a batch of buttery brioche bread out of the oven when she heard the sound of Jake's deep voice coming from the front room. She hadn't been expecting any other contractors or deliveries today. *Who could he be talking to?* Curious, she wiped her hands on her apron and peeked through the door. He was on his phone, one hand clasped on the back of his neck, pacing back and forth near the door, clearly agitated.

"It's not a good idea," Jake said into the phone, frustration evident in his voice.

Megan knew she shouldn't eavesdrop, but she was unable to make herself turn away.

"Look, I'm not pulling him out of school so you can take him to Disneyland," he said and stopped pacing. "I know he would have fun, but you could have taken him last month when you were supposed to have him, while he was on break, and I'm in the middle of a job." He was quiet for a minute while he listened, then ran his hand through his hair. "Yes, it would be nice if Spencer could have both of his parents together."

Jake turned and their eyes connected. Megan's cheeks flamed as she slipped back into the kitchen. She stepped over to the center island and dumped the bread loaves out of their pans and onto the cooling rack. *What was I thinking?* She should have backed out as soon as she saw he was on the phone.

She grabbed a towel off the island and threw it across the room, watching it land on the floor by the ovens. Jake's words echoed through her head, over and over. *Spencer should have both of his parents together.* What went on between him and Cindy was none of her business. *Then why did it bother me?*

Megan busied herself by cleaning the bread from the pans and gathering supplies to make a pate a choux dough. She wanted to test a new recipe for caramel éclairs and had mixed up the filling the day before. Working on a new recipe would require enough concentration to get Jake out of her head. *Right?*

She spooned the soft dough into a pastry bag and had just finished piping it onto large sheet pans when Jake entered the kitchen. Megan's stomach twisted as he approached her workspace, gazing at the pans with interest. *Why does he have to be so good looking?* He placed his hands on the island next to her and leaned forward, inspecting the tray with a quizzical expression on his face.

"What's that?"

He stood close enough that Megan could smell the clean, woodsy scent of his aftershave. Megan suddenly felt nervous even though—she rationalized—she had no reason to be. *Just friends, we're just friends,* she kept repeating in her mind. She could feel his eyes on her.

"It will be caramel éclairs," she said and turned to look at him. His close proximity had her stomach feeling like it was on a bad carnival ride.

"What's an éclair?"

Megan pointed to the strips of dough on the baking sheets. "These will bake up crisp on the outside and hollow in the center. Once they cool, I'll fill them with vanilla bean pastry cream. Then I'll drizzle them with caramel sauce and a little sprinkle of sea salt."

"Sounds fancy."

"I guess." Megan lifted one shoulder and glanced away. "I . . . I didn't mean to intrude on your call. I didn't know . . ." She trailed off, waving her hand in the direction of the door leading to the storefront.

Jake shrugged. "It's not a big deal."

"Everything okay?" Megan asked before she could stop herself. *It's not your business. Stay in your lane,* she chastised herself.

Jake turned so he was leaning back against the island and crossed his arms in front of his chest. He let out a long sigh. "Some people just don't like to be told no."

"Cindy?" she asked, even though she knew the answer.

He glanced at her out of the corner of his eye. "Yeah. She doesn't always think of what's best for Spencer first."

Megan chewed on her bottom lip. "I'm sorry," she said softly. She didn't know what it would be like to share custody of a child but couldn't imagine it would be easy. Especially with distance involved. Spencer was an amazing child. How he wouldn't come first was beyond her, but she didn't know the situation, either.

Jake turned his head and held her gaze for a long moment. A flicker of pain crossed his face. "This isn't how it was supposed to be."

The sadness and regret in his tone was almost palpable, and Megan's chest tightened. She didn't really want to hear him lament about his relationship with Cindy, but she wanted to be his friend. *Don't I? Yes, I do.* She began to fidget with the parchment liner on the sheet pan with her fingers.

"Spencer needs stability," he said wearily.

"I'm sure she'll come around," she replied, the words tasting sour as they came off her lips.

Jake's brows furrowed for a moment, and then he slowly shook his head. He straightened and placed his hand on hers. Heat radiated up her arm. He took a step toward her.

"I meant us, Megan. It was always supposed to be us."

Megan met his gaze. He was so close she could see tiny flecks of gold in his blue eyes. Everything she'd felt for him came flooding back as she stared into his eyes. She wasn't over him at all. Was he saying he wasn't over her, either? She opened her mouth to reply, but nothing came out. *Us?*

"Spencer adores you, you know?"

Megan nodded as though she was in a trance. "Me too . . . I mean, him." Her pulse raced and her face grew hot.

Jake lifted his hand and touched his thumb to her cheek. His gaze traveled to her lips, and she felt them tremble. He leaned forward. *Is he going to kiss me? Do I want him to? Yes. Wait, no!*

Megan's heart pounded so hard she was sure Jake could hear it. She heard his voice in her mind, telling Cindy over the phone how nice it would be for them to be a family again. She wouldn't let him hurt her again. Using every ounce of willpower she had, Megan took a quick step to the side and picked up the tray of éclairs.

"I should get these in the oven," she said, grateful

for the diversion. Her cheek still tingled where he had touched it, and she was sure her face was beet red. She hated that her body still responded to his touch. She hated even more that she still craved his touch.

She slid the baking tray into the oven and stepped back to the island, on the opposite side of where Jake stood. They stared at each other for a long moment.

He scrubbed his face with his hand. She could see the sadness and regret in his eyes. With a heaviness in her chest, she took a shaky breath.

"I'm really sorry, Megan," he murmured, shoving his hands into his pockets. Without another word, he turned and walked out of the room. She heard the door to the bakery open and close. He was gone.

"What do you mean, he almost kissed you?" Lacey set her cup of green tea down and leaned forward attentively.

"Not so loud," Megan chided, glancing around the coffee shop to see if anyone had overheard.

After Jake walked out of the bakery, she trashed her éclairs and sent an SOS message to Lacey to meet her at Brewed Awakening for some advice. They'd arrived at the same time and after placing their orders, they retreated to a corner table to talk. The coffee shop was bustling as usual, and Megan recognized Lucas as he rushed around bussing tables. Satisfied that no one was listening to their conversation, Megan turned back to her friend.

"It just sort of happened." She shrugged. "One minute we were talking, and the next he was . . . well, he leaned in, you know?"

"And?" She gestured for Megan to continue.

"I freaked out and grabbed the pan of éclairs." Megan covered her face with her hands and groaned, the fire in her cheeks hot under her fingers. She waved her hand in front of her.

Lacey sat back and started laughing. "You're kidding me, right?"

"No. I totally panicked." Megan took a sip of her latte and set it back on the table with a sigh.

"Why didn't you let him kiss you?"

Megan's head snapped up and her gaze locked with Lacey's. "It doesn't matter. He still has a thing for Cindy."

Lacey shook her head. "Not a chance. I saw how he looked at you at the church festival."

Megan frowned. She didn't want to think about the way he looked at her or the way it made her feel. "I heard him, Lacey." She spent the next few minutes filling Lacey in on the conversation she'd overheard at the bakery and what Jake had told her about Spencer.

Lacey was quiet for a moment as she processed the story. "I think you're wrong," she finally said. "You only heard one side of the conversation, Megan. You don't know what Cindy said to him."

"No, I don't. But I know what Jake said, and he's right. Spencer deserves to have a family."

"Not all families are made up of biological parents."

Megan wrinkled her nose. "Stop being so logical."

"Well, it's true. Look at my family. I love my step-dad just as much as I love my biological dad. It's like having a bonus parent. Plus, I *know* you still have a thing for him."

"Do not," Megan murmured, picking up her latte and taking a sip.

"Oh, come on." Lacey rolled her eyes. "You might tell yourself that, but I know better."

"I don't know." Megan looked down and slowly traced the edge of the heat sleeve on her cup with her finger. She recalled the message written on the cup she'd gotten the last time she was here. She yanked down the sleeve. *Everything that is, was first a dream.*

Lacey laughed and raised a brow. "What are you doing?"

"Did you ever notice these cups have sayings on them?"

"No?" Lacey lowered the cardboard sleeve on her cup. "There are signs everywhere, you just have to open your eyes," she read. "Interesting. What does yours say?"

Megan turned her cup so her friend could read it.

"That's pretty deep."

"I guess." Megan shrugged. "The one I got on my birthday said, 'Love is sweeter the second time aroun d.'"

Lacey raised a brow. "Now that *is* interesting."

Megan pulled the cardboard sleeve back into place and made a dismissive gesture with her hand. "It's a glorified fortune cookie. So, what's going on with Brian?"

"Who? Oh yeah. Brian." Lacey slumped in her chair. "Nothing. We broke up."

"What happened?"

"Nothing." Lacey shrugged. "That was the problem. There just weren't any . . . sparks. He didn't look at me the way Jake looks at you."

Megan rolled her eyes. "Oh, stop." She laughed. "You can't expect someone to look at you like that if you don't stay with them long enough to get to know them."

"I think you're wrong," Lacey countered. "I think when you find the right person, you just kind of . . . know. I just haven't found him yet."

The door to the coffee shop swung open. Megan watched with interest as Lacey's eyes grew wide and a pink tinge colored her cheeks. She turned and glanced over her shoulder to see who'd come in. It was Jake's friend, Shane Wickham. Had her friend been holding out on her?

"Hey, Shane!" she called, giving a little wave. "Come join us."

"Megan, what are you doing?" Lacey hissed. A stray strand of hair had escaped her messy bun, so she tucked it behind her ear.

Yep, there was definitely something going on here. Megan's lips curled into a wide grin as Shane approached their table.

"Afternoon, ladies." Shane greeted them with a smile. Megan noticed his gaze lingered a bit longer on Lacey.

He was an attractive man, although Megan had never given him a second glance. Her gaze bounced back and forth between Lacey and Shane. There was definitely a spark between them.

"Join us?" Megan asked again and broke off with a grunt when Lacey kicked her under the table.

"Wish I could," Shane said. "I just stopped in to grab some caffeine on my way to Missoula to catch a flight."

"Oh," Lacey frowned. "Where are you going?"

"Heading back to New York to finish a job." He glanced at his watch. "I better hit the road or I'm going to be late." He turned to Megan. "Great to see you and Jake together again."

Megan shook her head. "We aren't together," she said. "We're just friends."

Shane smirked. "That's what he said too." His gaze slid to Lacey and held there. Her face turned scarlet. "Lacey," he said, tipping his head in her direction. "Be seeing you." He turned and walked away, Lacey's gaze following him until he disappeared through the door.

"What's up with that?" Megan teased her friend.

Lacey fingered the edge of the cardboard sleeve on her cup and avoided meeting Megan's inquiring gaze. "Nothing is up with that."

Megan leaned forward. "You like him, don't you?"

"No," Lacey replied a little too quickly. She shrugged. "We talked a little at the church festival, that's all. Besides, he's still with Angie. Anyway . . . let's talk about you and Jake some more."

Megan pressed her lips together and gave a little shake of her head. "There *is* no me and Jake. We're just friends." She felt like a stuck record.

"You might think that, but you're different since you've been around him. You're happier. Your eyes light up every time his name is mentioned, Megan. Don't tell me you don't have feelings for him."

Megan let out a sigh. "I don't know. It's been nice spending time with him again. It almost seems like we were never apart. Then I remember what happened and . . . it's not that simple. He's got a family."

"Right, but I mean, he let his son spend time with you and get attached to you. He wouldn't do that if he wasn't still interested."

Megan thought about that for a minute. *Could Lacey be right?* She shrugged. "He did say Spencer adored me." She took another sip of her latte and chewed her lip. "I'm actually pretty attached to him, too," she admitted. "He's adorable."

Lacey slapped her hand down on the table. "See! A sign! Oh! And your cup said love is sweeter the second time around, right? Another sign!"

Megan laughed ruefully. "It's just not that easy, Lacey. And what about Cindy? I don't know."

Lacey reached across the table and grasped her hand. "God put him back in your life for a reason, Megan. Trust it."

Could she?

Chapter 9

JAKE FINISHED TIGHTENING THE last screw on the last shelf of the wooden display case he'd built and stepped back to survey his work. It was perfect. As he reached forward and brushed a stray bit of sawdust off the shelf, a bittersweet feeling came over him. His work in the bakery was nearly finished. He checked his watch. Megan should be arriving any minute now.

He carefully attached the large chalkboard menus on the wall behind the sales counter. He'd found some reclaimed wood to frame them, and Megan and Lacey had hand-lettered them with colored chalk. They looked amazing. He stared at the boards for a moment—at Megan's familiar handwriting—and thought of all the letters she'd written to him while he was away at college. He still had them in an old shoebox he kept in the attic. *Did I send her any?* He didn't think so. He usually called . . . when he could find the time. Jake closed his eyes and let out a long sigh. *If I could only go back in time. But then I wouldn't have Spencer.*

At first, it had been odd seeing her again and spending time with Megan. He'd been consumed with guilt. So many times over the past few years, he'd thought about what he would say if he came face to face with her again. But then they just seemed to fall back into the sort of friendship they'd always had. Comfortable and natural. And then he'd almost screwed it up again by trying to kiss her. *What was I thinking?* He had absolutely no willpower when it came to her, never had. He needed to think about Spencer, not try to relive the past.

The bell above the door jingled, and Jake almost sighed with regret. This would be the last day he'd get to spend with her. Whatever happened between the two of them, he was proud of the result of their working together.

"Hi, Jake," Megan said as she stepped into the room.

Jake turned and felt his heart skip a beat. She stood in the open doorway and smiled at him. The glow from the sun bathed her in light, almost making her look ethereal. An angel. His angel.

"Would you mind helping me carry some boxes in?" she asked, pulling him out of his trance.

"Of course," he replied. She could have asked him to lasso the moon and he would have rushed to buy a rope long enough to try.

They carried in several boxes and lined them up in front of the shelves he'd just finished. Megan dusted her hands together and looked at him, her eyes sparkling with excitement. Her hair was down today, the auburn locks falling over her shoulders. She wore a sage colored shirt that flowed over her hips. Faded denim jeans tucked into knee-high brown leather boots completed her casual outfit, and Jake thought she outshined any of the models he'd seen when he was in California. None of them had her warm heart, either, which only served to enhance her beauty.

"I can't wait to show you the shirts I got." She crouched next to one of the boxes and scraped at the edge of the packing tape with her fingernails.

Jake reached into his tool belt and pulled out a box cutter. He handed it to her, and their fingers brushed. He felt an electric jolt and pulled his hand back. Their eyes met and held for a long moment, and he wondered if she'd felt it too. She opened the box cutter and easily sliced through the tape on the box in front of her. Lifting the flaps, she pulled out a turquoise shirt and held it up. In white was an outline of a cupcake along with the words *A Little Something Sweet*. Megan held the shirt up to her shoulders, and a smile danced on her lips.

"What do you think?"

Jake's breath hitched and the words caught in his throat. He nodded his head while he tried to untie his tongue. "I love it," he finally managed.

Megan laid the shirt on top of the box and gestured toward the shelves. "These are perfect! I'll stack the shirts here, along with the coffee mugs in that box." She pointed to one of the boxes. "Mom is going to talk to some of her friends about bringing some items in to sell on consignment too."

Jake watched her talk animatedly about her plans and felt a warmth surge through him as he realized her dream had come full circle. And he'd helped her. Just like they always planned. He may have messed up the rest of their plans, but at least he'd gotten this part right. His grandpa used to say, you can't put a price on a dream fulfilled. He wondered if the rest of her dreams would include him too.

They did a walk through the bakery so she could sign off on his paperwork. Everything was in place, from the signage to the vintage pendant lights hanging over the display cases. Jake had made tables out of more reclaimed wood, and his mom had found some vintage iron cafe chairs that he refinished to go with them in the seating area. Another wood-framed chalkboard hung on the wall to the right of the display cases, where Megan could write the daily specials.

"I just can't believe it, Jake," Megan said, looking around the room one more time. They stood next to each other, and Jake found the smell of her perfume intoxicating.

"It's more than I could ever have imagined. Thank you." She turned and threw her arms around him.

He was momentarily taken off guard, but quickly recovered and wrapped his arms around her waist, returning her hug. She fit like she was molded to him. "It's just like we used to plan . . ." She trailed off and her eyes met his. She pulled away, her face tinged bright pink.

Jake clamped his lips together and took a deep breath before he nodded. "It is. Even better, I think." He wouldn't mess up this moment for her by reading into that hug and finding something that wasn't there. He fished the bakery key out of his pocket and held it out to her. "You'll be needing this back."

She took the key from his hand and stuck it in her pocket. "You do great work," she said, running her fingers along one of the tabletops. "I guess I never really expected you to be a business owner. You couldn't wait to get out of this town. It was always about baseball." She stared at him for a minute before continuing. "You really have a talent for this kind of work; I'm impressed."

Jake smiled warmly at the compliment. "Thank you. I think being in Los Angeles opened my eyes to a lot of things. Everything out there is so—" He paused, trying to find the words to explain. "Cookie cutter, I guess. Made me realize what I had always taken for granted." *In more ways than one*, he thought. "Things don't always work out the way we planned, I guess."

An emotion he couldn't identify flickered across her face, but as quickly as it had come, it vanished.

"No, they don't," she said softly.

"I think I'm where I'm supposed to be, though." He shoved his hands into his pockets. "Being here and working with my hands, I really enjoy it. Maybe it was growing up with all the antiques, but there's something sort of magical about being able to take something old and bring new life to it. Plus, Caribou Falls is a great town for Spencer to grow up in."

"Very true," she agreed. "And your folks are here. I'm sure they enjoy being able to see him often."

"Yeah, I don't know what I'd do without them."

They stood quietly for a minute. He wasn't ready to say goodbye. Not yet. He had an idea. "Let's celebrate."

She gave him a quizzical look and tucked a lock of hair behind her ear.

"Let's celebrate your bakery! Dinner at my house. I'll cook."

Megan grinned. "Sounds great, but I've seen you cook."

"What? Grilled cheese is cooking." He laughed.

"How about I cook," she said. "You still like lasagna?"

Jake closed his eyes and groaned. He loved lasagna. "You're on. But let me get the groceries."

She stuck out her hand. "Deal."

Pleased with himself for buying some extra time with her, he extended his hand and they shook on it. Megan made a list of items she would need, and she agreed to meet him at his place at five. She needed to run a few errands and check on her mom. That would give Jake plenty of time to pick up groceries, grab Spencer from school, and make sure the house was tidy.

He stopped by the market and found all of the items on Megan's list. He lingered in the wine aisle, debating on whether he should get wine to go with dinner or not. *Would that send the wrong message?* It wasn't a date, after all. Just two friends celebrating. Finally deciding it would be fine, he selected a bottle of Pinot Noir and after checking out, headed to the school to pick up Spencer.

"Dad, Josiah told me the best joke. I laughed so hard. Wanna hear it?" Spencer said as he climbed into his booster seat.

"Sure." Jake made sure he was secure before pulling away from the school.

"Why do giraffes have long necks?"

"I don't know, Spence. Why do they?"

"Because they have stinky feet." He giggled.

Jake glanced at Spencer through the rearview mirror and smiled. He remembered sitting with Shane at the same age, making up silly jokes and thinking they were the funniest kids in town. He was glad Spencer had a friend like that.

"Whoa, you bought lots of food," Spencer said, noticing the pile of grocery bags next to him. "Is Grandma and Grandpa coming over?"

"No, I invited Megan to come over."

"Like a date?"

He wished. "No, she's going to make us supper."

"Like a date," Spencer insisted. "What is she making? It looks like you bought everything at the store."

"Lasagna. And not a date. We're celebrating finishing the work at her bakery."

"But it could be a date."

"It's not a date, Spencer."

"I like Megan. She's really pretty. Don't you think she's pretty, Dad?"

"Yes, she is."

"Then it should be a date. Did you get her flowers? The man always gives the lady flowers on TV when it's a date."

"Spencer, it's not a date." Jake let out an exasperated sigh. Maybe letting him spend so much time with Megan wasn't a good idea. Now that the work at the bakery was finished, their afternoons together would likely come to a halt. Unless . . .

"You need to get her flowers, Dad. It's the right thing to do." Spencer's voice interrupted his thoughts. As much as he hated to admit it, and likely wouldn't admit it, his son was right. She should have flowers.

"All right, all right," he acquiesced. "Let's stop and get her flowers."

"I told you it was a date."

Chapter 10

MEGAN TURNED ONTO SECOND Street and made her way down the block toward the house Jake now owned. She'd been enchanted with the two-story Victorian ever since she could remember. As a child, she'd walked past it on her way to the library and would often stop at the park across the street to sit and stare at it, dreaming about what it would be like to live in such a fine house rather than the small rambler her parents owned.

Caribou Falls had a number of beautiful Victorian homes, but this one was always special to her for some reason. Once she and Jake started dating, she shared that dream with him. They would talk for hours about how they would one day own it and raise their own family in it.

She pulled up in front of the majestic house and drew in a breath. It was even more beautiful than she remembered. The house—formerly a dull green color—was now painted brilliant white with black trim. Grand white pillars adorned the wraparound porch, and Megan could see a wooden porch swing hanging in one corner. The front door was painted a dark sage green, and meticulously trimmed bushes lined the front of the home.

Megan recalled what Pastor Richard had said about new beginnings, and she vowed to be happy that both their dreams had come true. She got her bakery, and he got the house. Shaking her head, she tried to clear her thoughts. She carefully lifted a pastry box from the passenger seat and climbed out of her car.

A flutter of butterflies danced in her stomach as she rapped on the door. As footsteps approached from the other side, she painted on a smile, unsure why she felt anxious about being here. She smoothed her blouse and wished she'd taken the time to change clothes or at least put on lipstick. *It's not a date*, she chastised herself as the door opened and she met Spencer's smiling face.

"Megan!" he exclaimed and ran forward, throwing his arms around her legs.

"Hi, Spencer," she replied and tousled his soft blond curls.

He grabbed her hand and pulled her into the house. "Dad, she's here!" He began pulling her toward a grand staircase. The refinished wood gleamed, and a stained-glass window sent refracted prisms throughout the entry. It looked just as she had imagined it would.

"I want to show you my room!" Spencer said, and Megan smiled at the excitement in the child's voice.

Jake walked into the entryway, and the butterflies in Megan's stomach reawakened. He'd changed out of his faded work clothes and into a pair of dark denim jeans and a slate blue Henley, which made his eyes look even more blue. He had shaved, and his still slightly damp hair curled up along the edges. The man was gorgeous.

"Hold on, buddy," he said to Spencer. "Let her get in the door." Turning his attention to Megan, he gave her a smile that could stop traffic. The kind that could melt hearts. The kind that used to melt hers. Judging by the feeling in her chest, it still had that effect.

"Hi, Megan. Sorry about my overly excited son." He put his hand on Spencer's shoulder.

Spencer shrugged it off. "She *is* in the door, Dad. Can I *please* show her my room?"

Jake rolled his eyes, shot her an apologetic smile, and waved toward the staircase. "Go on, but bring her back to the kitchen when you're done or we're never going to have her famous lasagna."

Megan laughed and allowed herself to be pulled toward the staircase by the small child. "Famous? You have high expectations," she said over her shoulder as they climbed the stairs.

"No, I have a good memory," he called from below.

Smiling, Megan followed Spencer down the hallway and into his bedroom. Posters of airplanes and a space shuttle covered the light blue walls. A large wooden bunk bed with a built-in desk took up most of one wall. Shelves full of books and toys lined another wall, and two giant bean bag chairs sat atop a thick rug to complete the play area.

"Isn't it awesome?" Spencer asked, smiling proudly.

"It's very awesome. I love your bunk bed."

"Yeah, me too. This way, Josiah has his own bed so he can stay over sometimes." He ran toward the shelves and carefully lifted a model airplane off them. He gingerly held it out so she could see it better. "Look what Dad helped me make. I love airplanes."

Megan studied the airplane and thought of all the time and patience it must have taken for the two of them to assemble the intricate model. "That's quite a project."

"It took us a long time to make it. We're going to do a space shuttle next."

"That sounds like a lot of fun."

"Mmm hmm. Maybe you can help us." He carefully set the model back in its spot on the shelves and turned to her. He eyed the pastry box in her hand as if just noticing it. "Hey, what's in the box?"

"It's a surprise for after supper."

"Oh! I love surprises. Is it something sweet?" Spencer gazed at her expectantly.

Megan felt another tug at her heart, only this was different. She was falling in love with the little boy. She reached out with her hand and touched his soft cheek. "What do you think?"

He grinned. "I think it is."

"I think you're right. Now, let's go find your dad so I can make you some lasagna."

"Yay! I love lasagna!"

Megan chuckled and followed him back downstairs, through the living room, and into the kitchen. The living room was large, with beautifully refinished wood floors, white-trimmed windows, doors, and baseboards, and impossibly high ceilings. The walls were painted dove grey, and a cozy fireplace filled one corner. An overstuffed, dark grey sectional sofa took up most of the living space, and a large flat screen television was attached to the opposite wall. Open

French doors led into the kitchen and dining area.

Her eyes widened as she stepped into the kitchen. The floor's soft-grey ceramic tiles complimented the veining in the white marble countertops. The cabinets were painted a beautiful, soft sage green, and white subway tiles lined the backsplash. A white farmhouse sink sat in front of a large window overlooking the backyard, and he'd installed high-end stainless steel appliances. A large pantry sat off to one side, and there was a small seating area near the sliding glass patio door that led onto a deck in the backyard. If she had designed it herself, she wouldn't have changed a thing.

"Did he give you the full tour?" Jake asked. He stood on the other side of the long counter, an array of pans and groceries set out in front of him.

Megan smiled. "He did. He even showed me the model airplane you built with him."

"She's gonna help us with the space shuttle, Dad!" Spencer said, climbing onto one of the stools that lined the counter.

"Is she?" Jake grinned, shooting Megan a questioning glance.

She shrugged her shoulders. "Might be fun," she said, noncommittally. "I absolutely love what you've done with this house. You really have a great eye for detail."

"Oh, stop. You're going to make me blush," Jake quipped. "I'm glad you like it, though."

"Like it? I love it. It's . . . perfect." She set the pastry box on the edge of the counter and walked around to the other side.

"What's in the box?" Jake asked, reaching for it.

Megan playfully slapped his hand away. "You'll have to wait and see."

"She said it's a surprise," Spencer said. "A little something sweet, just like the bakery! But we have to eat first. When are you gonna make supper, Megan? I'm hungry."

"You're always hungry, Spence." Jake laughed.

"I'm a growing boy. That's what Grandma says."

They laughed.

"That you are, Spencer," Megan said as she surveyed the groceries Jake had set out on the counter. "Looks like everything is here. Let's get started."

"Can I help?" Spencer asked.

"Of course. I'll let you sprinkle on the cheese."

Jake browned the Italian sausage while Megan prepared the sauce. They chatted about Spencer's day at school and the renovation project Jake would soon be starting. It felt so natural and so right being there with them. *It feels like family.* Megan thought again about what her friend Lacey had said about her and Jake. *She was right*, Megan thought. *Can I give him another chance? Could we be a family?*

Spencer helped sprinkle the last of the cheese on top of the lasagna, and Jake slid it into the oven. He offered his son a quick smile.

"It has to bake for about an hour. Why don't you watch TV for a little while so Megan and I can visit?"

Spencer nodded vigorously and climbed off the stool. He paused in the doorway to the living room. "Don't forget to give her the date flowers, Dad." He grinned and disappeared into the other room.

"Date flowers?" Megan raised her eyebrows and watched with interest as Jake's cheeks began to flush. He reached into a bag on the opposite counter and pulled out a small bouquet of pink and white daisies.

"He insisted this was a date and we needed to get you flowers." A smile played on his lips as he extended the flowers to her.

She took them, held them up to her nose, and smelled their sweet aroma. "I love daisies."

"I remember," he said softly. He pulled a tall drinking glass from one of the upper cabinets and filled it with water. "I don't have a vase, but you can put them in this glass for now."

Megan pulled the cellophane wrapper off the bouquet and arranged them in the glass. "They are by far the best date flowers I've ever received. I'll have to remember to thank him."

"I see how it is." He laughed. "I buy the flowers, and he gets the credit."

She smirked and threw him a wink before turning back to the counter to assemble the salad. "He's really a special kid," she said as she diced the tomatoes.

"Yeah, I'm pretty lucky."

"You're a great dad, Jake," Megan glanced at him, holding his gaze for a moment before turning back to the vegetables. "I always knew you would be."

"Thanks, Meg," he said. "I, uh . . ." He shifted and cleared his throat but didn't continue.

Megan stopped chopping and looked at him, waiting for him to finish. She couldn't miss the color that crept into his face from his neck. She wondered what had him so tongue tied. He looked like a kid who had just been caught with frosting on his hands.

He opened his mouth, then with a slight furrow of his brow, he closed it and let out a sigh. He turned and opened a cabinet before meeting her gaze. "Would you like some wine?"

"I'd love that, thanks," she replied and turned back to chopping vegetables while Jake opened and poured the wine. She filled the bowl with romaine lettuce and the chopped tomatoes, then added some chopped pecans, blueberries, and a sprinkle of green onions and feta cheese. She then drizzled it with a raspberry vinaigrette and tossed the whole thing with bamboo salad forks.

"That looks amazing," Jake said, handing her a goblet.

"Thanks." She reached for the glass, and their hands brushed. The jolt was so jarring, she almost dropped it. They locked eyes, and the feeling that coursed through her was as electric as it had ever been.

He took a step toward her, and she tightened her grip on the glass. Her breath quickened. She turned to face him with her back against the counter. Her eyes traveled to his full lips, and she was overcome with a longing to feel them on her own. He was so close, she could feel his warm breath in her hair.

"Megan, I—" he began, his voice deep and husky.

"Shh," she said and lifted her mouth to his, her lips barely brushing against his.

She could hear a sharp intake of breath but wasn't sure if it was him or her. His hands settled on her waist and pulled her closer as his lips pressed against hers, more firmly this time. She closed her eyes and lost herself in the kiss.

"Dad, I'm thirsty."

Spencer's voice registered in her brain, and Jake took a quick step away from her, causing her to nearly spill her wine. She turned, set the goblet down, and held on to the counter to steady her weak knees just as Spencer appeared in the kitchen.

"Is dinner almost ready? I'm going to starve to death."

Megan smiled and watched Jake hand Spencer a glass of water.

"I hardly think you're going to starve," he said. "Why don't you help me set the table? It should be ready by then." He glanced at her for confirmation.

She nodded and was rewarded with a warm smile.

"We'll get back to where we left off later," he promised quietly, his eyes shining with more than mischief.

Her cheeks grew hot as she imagined being in his arms again. She turned away and took a sip of her wine before giving the salad one last toss.

Spencer eyed the bowl on the counter and grimaced. "Ewww! Salad is for rabbits. I'm not a rabbit."

"Spencer." Jake tried to suppress a chuckle. "Don't be rude."

"That's what Josiah says. That salads are for rabbits."

"Well, this salad is astronaut approved." Megan smiled. Out of the corner of her eye she saw Jake nod with approval, a smirk lifting the corners of his mouth.

Spencer eyed her skeptically. "Really?"

"Cross my heart," she said. *I could really get used to this.*

Their banter was interrupted by the sound of the doorbell. She looked at Jake and saw a confused expression cross his face.

He shrugged. "Probably just one of the neighbor kids," he said.

"I'll get it," Spencer cried out and ran from the room.

Megan heard the sound of the door open and then Spencer's voice saying, "Mom!"

The tips of her fingers went numb, and she felt the color drain from her face. Her breath caught in her throat, and she couldn't breathe. *Did I hear him right?* One look at the tightness in Jake's eyes confirmed she had. *Cindy.*

Chapter 11

J AKE'S STOMACH CLENCHED. SURELY he misheard what Spencer said. He looked at Megan. Her face had gone pale, and her wide eyes searched his for an explanation. She'd heard the same thing. He could hear Spencer chatting excitedly, but the sound of approaching high heels clicking on the hardwood floors drowned out his words. He suddenly felt lightheaded and closed his eyes. *This can't be happening.* Things were going so perfectly.

"Jake, darling," Cindy purred as she walked into the kitchen. "I'm home."

He forced his eyes to open. Cindy stood in the doorway of the kitchen, wearing a tight, short white skirt and snug blouse to match. White sandals with impossibly high heels completed the ensemble. She looked as though she'd just stepped out of a magazine. Her hair—usually blonde but now bleached almost white—was cut short in a style that framed her perfectly made-up face. A pair of sunglasses dangled from one hand, and a stack of thin, gold bracelets dangled from the other that gripped the handle of her luggage.

It just keeps getting worse. He tried to speak, but the words wouldn't come. It was like his brain had frozen.

The timer on the oven buzzed. Jake looked at Megan. He could see the anguish in her eyes and knew he would lose her again. He couldn't let that happen. Before he could figure out what to say, she walked to the stove, turned the timer off, and pulled the lasagna out of the oven.

"Megan made lasagna for us," Spencer said, oblivious to the tension around him.

"Isn't that sweet," Cindy said in a sing-song voice. Her eyebrow raised with amusement, and a cold smile that didn't quite reach her eyes popped onto her face.

"Dinner is ready," Megan said, and Jake could hear

the coldness in her voice. "You'll have to serve your-selves." She threw him a frosty look, pulled the oven mitts off her hands, tossed them on the counter, and walked away.

"Megan, wait," Jake finally managed, but it was too late.

She held up her hand. "I'll see myself out," she said over her shoulder. "Enjoy your meal."

"Aren't you going to eat with us, Megan?" Spencer asked.

"No, Spencer. I think your table is plenty crowded already." She stopped long enough to place a quick kiss on the boy's cheek. "Be good for your dad, okay?"

Spencer nodded sadly. "I wish you didn't have to leave. I want you to stay for dinner . . . and for al-ways."

"I have to go, buddy. Goodbye." Her voice cracked as the words came out of her mouth, and Jake's heart twisted in his chest. She stepped around Cindy and was gone. The sound of the door closing a few seconds later echoed in his head. What a disaster.

"Well, seems like I came just in time." Cindy cast

a pointed look at Jake.

The room seemed to spin for a second. Images of the sadness in Spencer's eyes, pink and white daisies, the bubbling pan of lasagna, Megan's half-empty glass of wine, and Cindy's saccharine smile tumbled around his head in a blur. He closed his eyes for a moment and took a deep breath.

"Cindy, what are you doing here? How did you find the house?" Jake asked, barely able to control his tone. He didn't want to create an even bigger scene in front of Spencer.

Cindy glanced at her nails and shrugged one shoulder. "It wasn't hard. My lawyer knew where you were. And I told you, I've come . . . home. Let's eat this wonderful dinner your . . . who is she? Your nanny prepared. It smells delicious, although I'll have to skip the lasagna. Too many carbs." She patted her flat stomach and blinked innocently at him.

"Are you going to stay here now, Mom?" Spencer asked. Jake didn't miss the unmistakable sound of disappointment in his son's voice.

"No, she's not," he said before Cindy had a chance

to respond. She opened her mouth to argue, but Jake shot her a look and she wisely stayed quiet. "She's just here for a visit. A *short* visit."

Appeased, Spencer smiled. "I'm hungry, Dad. Can we eat?"

Torn between his desire to run after Megan and set things right and trying to get through the evening without further upsetting his son, Jake decided he would have to smooth things over with Megan later. He hoped it wouldn't be too late, but he needed to deal with Cindy first.

"Sure, Spence. Let's eat."

They sat at the table and ate a tense meal. Spencer was the only one that seemed to be enjoying himself. As he chatted about school and airplanes, Jake watched Cindy half listen to him while she picked at the salad on her plate. Every opportunity she had, she would tell another story about what it was like being on a real movie set. It was clear she wasn't interested in what Spencer was trying to say, and the child fell quiet while he finished his plate. She continued talking, happy to be the center of attention.

The lasagna was delicious, but Jake could barely choke down the small piece he'd taken. He'd finally managed to make things right with Megan, and he blew it again. Because of Cindy. *No*, he thought. Because of him. He should have gone after her immediately. Sent Cindy away. But he couldn't do that in front of Spencer.

He pushed his plate away. Dessert was forgotten and Spencer was excused to play in his room so Jake could have some time alone with Cindy.

Jake put the leftovers in the fridge and loaded the dishwasher while Cindy sat at the counter and watched. She didn't offer to help. Cleaning wasn't her thing. Cooking wasn't, either. Come to think of it, Jake wasn't able to come up with anything that was, besides maybe hair and makeup. How had he been so blind? And foolish? His mother was right. He never should have married her. He'd never loved her; it had always been about Spencer. Now he couldn't understand what she was doing in his house.

"What are you doing, Cindy?" He leaned against the counter and crossed his arms over his chest.

"I already told you." She smiled demurely and looked up at him from under her long, heavily mascaraed eyelashes. "I'm back. I've missed you and Spencer."

He wasn't buying it. "What happened? Were you passed over for the part in the movie? Did what's-his-name . . . Eric, get tired of you and move on?" He knew his words were harsh, but he was tired of playing her games.

She frowned and slid off the stool, her mouth forming a perfectly choreographed pout as she walked around the counter and stopped in front of him. Up close, he could see fine lines under her makeup. She looked tired and older than her twenty-seven years. She lifted her hand and ran a manicured nail down the center of his chest and smiled coyly at him.

"That doesn't really matter," she said. "I'm here now, and I'm staying this time."

He grabbed her hand, moved it back down to her side, and took a step away from her. "It does matter, Cindy."

She rolled her eyes and huffed out a breath. "Fine."

Her upper lip curled, and she hopped onto the counter, kicking off her shoes. "They cut my part. They said it wasn't important enough. And his name is Aaron, not Eric. And I dumped him. Satisfied?"

Aaron was the latest man in her life, and Jake was surprised he'd lasted as long as he had.

"It's not about being satisfied, Cindy. It's about what you're really doing here."

"Don't you see? It's all a sign that this is where I should be," she simpered. "I can learn to live in this . . . small town and old house." She lifted her hand and twirled her wrist. "I can get used to working at that shop your parents have. I can even accept that I'll never be more than a wife and mother."

"You're hiding out." He pinned her with his eyes until she looked away. He raked his fingers through his hair and blew out a long breath. "If you stay here, you'll be settling." He stepped in front of where she sat and placed his finger gently under her chin, turning her head so she faced him. He held her gaze for a long moment before she glanced away. "And so will I." He dropped his hand back to his side. "I want someone who will be a true partner in my life, not someone who settles for me. Relationships are hard enough without having such low expectations, don't you think?"

She looked at him but didn't say anything.

"You deserve that too, Cindy. A true partner in life." He stepped away and leaned back against the counter across from her. "Besides, Spencer needs stability. It's not fair to him if you tell him you're going to stay and then leave when you get tired of being here. You don't want to be here, and you know it. There's no great love story with us. There never was, never will be."

"She's not your nanny, is she?" Cindy sniffed.

"No, she's not."

"I should probably go, then." She looked at the floor. Jake could tell she was hedging for an invitation.

"You can't stay here, Cindy."

"I know." She let out a long breath. "You're right. I'm hiding out." She looked up again, tears welling in her eyes. She carefully wiped them away with her manicured fingers.

Jake handed her a tissue and watched while she blotted her face. He wasn't sure what to say. He'd stopped trying to figure her out a long time ago.

"I don't know why I even broke up with him," she confessed, staring into space. "He's actually not a bad guy, you know?" Her gaze shifted to him. "I was just upset about not getting the part." She sniffled and shrugged. "I didn't think he felt sorry enough for me, so I started a fight. Can you imagine?" She lifted her hands in a helpless gesture and let out a rueful little laugh.

"Yeah, actually I can." He chuckled and shook his head. It was so like her to do that. She'd done it with him several times during the short time they were married.

"Yeah, I may have done that to you too," she admitted. "Did I hear Spencer say that woman's name was Megan?"

Jake nodded. Megan had always been a sore spot with her. Cindy was very possessive. Even if she didn't necessarily want what she had, if it was hers, she didn't want anyone else to have it.

"*The* Megan?"

He nodded again. She'd heard all about Megan from his mother while they were married. It had been one of many points of contention for them.

Cindy was quiet for a minute and then nodded her head too. "She's pretty, in a brown paper bag sort of way."

He smirked. That was the closest thing to a compliment she would ever give.

"So, what are you going to do? I can find you a room at the motel if you want," he gently offered. As messed up as her intentions were, he wasn't about to turn her out with no place to stay, but he was anxious to find Megan.

"Let me call a cab and then I'll say goodbye to Spencer. I can catch a flight back to L.A. tomorrow. That will give me time to have a long talk with Aaron." She paused for a moment before sliding off the counter and slipping her feet back into her shoes. She touched his arm and then reached for the phone in her bag. "I hope things work out with Megan."

Jake nodded. "Thanks, Cindy. I hope things work

out with Aaron."

"Oh, they will." She grinned, her voice full of confidence once again. "He'd be a fool to let me go."

Jake laughed. He felt good about their conversation. He didn't think she'd ever really change, but hopefully he gave her something to think about. She deserved to find someone too. *Speaking of someone . . .* He pulled his phone out of his pocket and hit speed dial.

"Mom, I need a favor."

Thirty minutes later, Cindy was well on her way to the airport in a taxi, his mom was watching a movie with Spencer, and Jake was backing out of the driveway in his truck. He had tried calling Megan several times, but her phone went straight to voicemail each time. His stomach rolled as he drove through town toward A Little Something Sweet.

The bakery was dark inside, and he didn't see her little red car parked in front. He drove around to check the alley, but it wasn't there either. Where was she? He headed toward her mom's house.

The driveway was empty, but he pulled up and put his truck in park anyway. *Her car could be in the garage*, he reasoned. He knocked on the door, and it seemed an eternity before her mother answered it.

"Jake," she said, clearly surprised to see him. "What can I do for you?"

"Hi, Mrs. Turner, is Megan here? I need to talk to her." His palms felt moist, and his heart was pounding so hard, he was sure she could hear it.

Her brow furrowed. "I thought she was with you." The confusion on her face quickly turned to concern. "Is everything ok?"

"It will be," he promised and ran back to his truck. He sat for a minute, his fingers drumming on the steering wheel, trying to think where she would be. Then it hit him. He put the truck in reverse and backed out of the driveway.

Chapter 12

MEGAN STOOD ON THE footbridge over Hanging Horn Creek and watched the water rushing below her. The burbling sound of the current moving over the rocks had always served to soothe her in the past, but it had little effect this evening.

As a child, her dad would bring her to Caribou Lake National Park. They would hike this trail to where the old Lambert's Trading Post used to be and picnic while her mom played bridge with her friends. It was their special time. The hike up to the old trading post was always fun, but somehow the hike back seemed to take twice as long. The footbridge where she stood was only a short distance from the parking lot, and it was here she would get her second wind. She remembered standing in this same spot with her dad many times, watching the water and talking about anything and everything. When she was a little older, she'd ride her bike here with Jake, and they would sit on the edge of the bridge with their feet dangling over the water and talk.

Jake.

The lump in her throat grew thicker, and the water below blurred as her eyes filled with fresh tears. How she wished her dad was here right now to talk to her. To tell her what to do. To let her cry on his large, soft shoulder. She recalled her dad telling her that this was a special place. That if you listened hard enough, you could hear God talking to you. After he died, she'd come here many times, hoping to hear God. She watched as a tear fell from her cheek, and her eyes followed it until it landed in the creek. The water moved so fast, it didn't even leave a ripple. Its insignificance to the volume of the creek mirrored the insignificance she felt in her soul.

What had she been thinking? Why did she think

it could work between them a second time? *Love is sweeter the second time around*, the strange writing on the cup had said, but this didn't feel very sweet. This hurt.

Hot tears rolled down her cheeks, and she swiped them away. She should have known better. She *heard* him on the phone with Cindy. It couldn't be a coincidence that she showed up at his house *with luggage* just days later. She felt like such a fool. But it seemed so right with him. It felt like family. How could it be wrong?

Lord, please show me what my path is, she prayed. *Still my troubled heart. I give You all my worries and concerns. Help me know when to stop and listen for Your direction.*

Megan could see the vibrant pink and orange colors of the sun low in the sky through the pines. She'd have to leave soon, before it got dark, or she wouldn't be able to see the trail. Megan closed her eyes and listened to the sound of small animals scurrying around before settling in for the night and the soft breeze blowing through the pine needles. The sound of approaching footsteps and a snapping twig made her eyes pop open. Her body tensed, and she held her breath as the steps got closer.

A familiar figure appeared on the trail. *Jake*. She felt a mixture of relief and trepidation as he approached. Perspiration shone on his brow. Had he run the half-mile distance to the bridge from the parking lot?

"You're here," he breathed, stopping next to her. His eyes had a haunted look to them.

"What are you doing here, Jake? Shouldn't you be with Cindy?" The words tasted bitter in her mouth, and she swallowed hard as she saw the flicker of pain cross his eyes.

"Cindy's gone," he said. "She's on her way back to L.A."

"She's not staying?" She slid him a guarded look.

"No. She never was. I tried to tell you."

"But I thought . . ." She trailed off.

"There's nothing between me and Cindy," he said, his eyes desperately searching hers for understanding. "There never was, Megan. It never should have happened."

Megan's breath bottled up in her chest as she listened to him and chewed on her bottom lip. *What is he saying?*

He drew in a long breath and scrubbed his jaw with his hand. "I thought I'd lose Spencer if I didn't marry her. I never meant to hurt you." He took a step closer to her. "I made so many mistakes. I never thought I'd have a chance to make it up to you. But then there was the bakery, and you were there, and it was like . . . it was like we'd never been apart."

Megan's stomach fluttered, and a chill spread through her. She rubbed her arms. Jake slipped his denim jacket off and draped it around her shoulders. She closed her eyes for a moment as its warmth soaked through her. The smell of him filled her senses. Was this the sign she asked God for? She opened her eyes and found him staring at her intently. A soft warmth glowed in his eyes.

"How did you know I'd be here?"

"I remember this was always your special place." He smiled gently. "I always thought of it as our special place, too."

Her brows furrowed for a moment, then she remembered. "This is the first place you kissed me."

"I remember. I hoped that kiss would go on forever." He stepped in front of her, taking her hands in his. "Megan, when I think back to when we were kids growing up together, I can remember so many things, but for the life of me, I can't remember a single time when I wasn't in love with you."

Megan's cheeks burned, her heart hammered in her chest, and tears welled in her eyes. She struggled to find the right words.

"I wish you'd say something," he said.

"I wish you'd kiss me." She wrapped her arms around his waist and pulled him to her.

"More than happy to give the lady what she wants," he replied, a grin appearing on his handsome face. "I love you, Megan Turner," he said as he lowered his lips to hers.

When Jake finally released her, Megan caught her breath and looked into his deep blue eyes.

"What do you say?" he asked.

Megan touched her lips hesitantly. That was some kiss. She could barely think. "About what?"

"You, me, and Spence." He raised an eyebrow. "Becoming a family?"

A family. She wanted that more than anything, but could she trust him again? "I want to, Jake," she said softly, "but I'd be lying if I said I wasn't scared after everything that happened."

Jake stared at her for a moment. "I don't want to look in the past. I want to look to the future." He reached up and cupped her chin in his hands. "And right now, I'm looking at my future. I know I made mistakes, Megan, but I promise you I'll spend the rest of my life making it up to you if you give me the chance."

Megan let out a squeal and jumped into his arms, wrapping her arms around his neck. "I love you, Jake Sullivan," she said.

Unable to wait another second, Jake slanted his mouth over hers and kissed her. Her soft lips molded perfectly to his, and she pressed into him until he could barely stand on his own. He kissed her with all the hunger and longing he'd had bottled up inside him, and the kiss grew more demanding until they finally broke apart, both of them breathless.

"I love you, Megan," he said and took her hand, leading her back to where they parked their cars.

"Let's go start our future."

Epilogue

"WELCOME TO BREWED AWAKENING. How can I help you today?" Paul asked as Megan stepped up to the counter. "You want your regular latte?"

"Hi, Paul." She smiled. "No, today I'll take a ginger mint herb tea, please. For here."

Paul lifted his eyebrows in surprise but didn't say anything as he rang up her order. "Just take a seat," he said, handing Megan her change. "I'll have Lucas bring it out to you. Have a great day."

"Thanks, Paul. You too." She stuck the change in her purse and took a seat at a table near the door. She glanced at her phone to check the time. *Jake and*

Spencer should be arriving any minute. She set the phone back on the table and couldn't help admiring the stunning ring that now adorned her left hand. The princess-cut diamond sparkled in the sunlight shining through the window behind her, sending prisms of rainbows dancing across the table.

Right after school let out for the summer, she and Jake had taken Spencer to Disneyland. They decided to elope while they were there, and Megan still felt like pinching herself to make certain it wasn't all just a dream. Cindy was able to fit some time in her schedule to see Spencer, and they had a few blissful days alone to honeymoon on the beach.

The bakery was flourishing. After a successful grand opening, the shop had remained busy. Megan had just hired a full-time baker so she would be able to leave in time to get Spencer after school, now that it had started again. Ann had recovered, and her cancer was in full remission. She helped out at the shop most days and loved her new role as Grandma to Spencer. Between her and Roger and Cathy, there was no shortage of attention for him.

The door to the coffee shop opened, and Megan glanced over to see who it was. A woman and her friend walked in and went to the counter. She took a deep breath, trying to calm herself. Just then, Lucas walked up to the table and carefully set the mug of tea in front of Megan.

"Thanks, Lucas." She smiled at the young man.

"Need honey?" he asked, wiping his hands on his apron.

"No, thanks."

"Okay. Bye, then." He turned and began walking away. "Everything is just right," she heard him say as he disappeared around the corner.

The door opened again, and this time, she saw Jake and Spencer enter the cafe. She waved them over and felt butterflies begin dancing in her stomach.

"Hi, Mom," Spencer said, climbing onto the chair next to hers and leaning into her shoulder.

"Hey, Spence. How was your day?" She wrapped her arm around him and glanced at Jake, who sat in the chair across from her, a concerned expression on his face. She winked at her handsome husband and turned her attention back to her son. Spencer had immediately insisted on calling her Mom, saying that he was very lucky now to have not just one, but two moms. Megan couldn't love him more if she had given birth to him.

"It was great. I love my new teacher, and guess what?" He grinned, revealing a missing tooth.

"You lost your tooth!" she exclaimed and tousled his blond curls. "We'll have to stop and get some ice cream on the way home to celebrate."

"How was your appointment?" Jake cut in. He reached across the table and took Megan's hands in his. "Is everything okay?"

She had left the bakery earlier than usual that day to attend a doctor's appointment. She hadn't been feeling well for several weeks, and Jake insisted she get checked out.

"We're just fine," she beamed.

Jake's eyes widened and his whole face lit up. "We?"

She nodded and placed a hand on her belly. "We're having a baby."

"You mean I get to be a big brother?" Spencer asked.

"Yes, and you are going to be the best big brother ever," she replied.

Jake slid his chair back and stepped around the table so he could pull her into his arms. "I love you so much, Megan."

"I love you too, Jake."

* * *

I hope you enjoyed A Little Something Sweet. Please consider leaving a review – reviews help not only the author, but other readers as they select their next book.

Continue reading for a free preview of Laura's novel, Royally Unexpected.

Royally Unexpected
Chapter One - Preview

THERE HAD TO BE *more to life than this.*

The roar from the cannons was deafening. Prince Dorian Tennesley let out a long sigh and tried not to fidget as he stood at attention for the royal salute. Once the cannons were quiet, his mother, Queen Sophia, reigning monarch of Avington, waved to her subjects. The park in central Avington was filled with men, women, and children. Dorian's eye twitched as the crowd erupted with cheers and applause.

What did people find so entertaining about seeing his family? Dorian never understood the fascination. He couldn't remember a time he wasn't being hounded by fans or paparazzi. To him, it was all pomp and circumstance, and he was tired of it. As the second son, and fourth in line to the throne, it wasn't like his appearance there mattered. But his mother insisted. "It's your duty," she'd admonished when he'd told her he wasn't interested. *Duty, obligation, responsibility.* It didn't matter which word she used, it all amounted to the same thing—a life that wasn't his own.

Today's ceremony was to honor the President of Ireland's arrival in the small island country of Avington and marked the third such visit in as many months. The sun shone brightly, and a cool breeze floated in off the sea, ruffling a wisp of hair off his forehead. Dorian's mind wandered as the queen introduced the visiting president.

Dorian scanned the crowd and settled his gaze on a pretty woman standing next to a large hawthorn tree. She stared back at him and shot him a seductive grin. His eyebrows twitched, and he fought to keep his expression neutral. She raised a slender arm and wiggled her fingers at him before pressing them to her cherry red lips and blowing him a kiss. Someone softly cleared their throat next to him, and Dorian suppressed a groan. *Philip.* He slid a glance to the right and met his older brother's icy glare. Before Dorian could react, the throng of onlookers broke into a roar of applause and Philip turned to follow the queen toward the waiting carriages that would take them through town and back to the castle.

Dorian's gaze flicked back to the hawthorn tree, but the woman was no longer there. Heaving a sigh, he turned and proceeded toward the rest of their entourage. The royal carriages were made of fine wood, their panels painted in forest green with carved wood and gilt moldings. The doors were emblazoned with the Avington royal arms. Ornamental brass and crystal lamps adorned the four corners of each carriage's body, and they were upholstered in fine chestnut leather. The hoods were folded back, and two uniformed footmen sat in each rumble. A postilion guided each team of black Friesian horses.

The queen paused and gave the crowd a final wave before climbing into the first of two horse-drawn carriages, alongside the visiting president and his wife. Dorian climbed into the second carriage with his brother Philip, Philip's wife Anna, and his one-year-old nephew Archer. Archer squealed and pointed at the horses, and some of the tension left Dorian's shoulders as he smiled at the youngster. He loved his nephew, loved kids really, but wasn't sure he saw them in his future. Kids meant marriage. Dorian shuddered at the thought.

Mounted soldiers from the Avington Cavalry escorted the two carriages out of Battenburg Park and they wound their way through the streets of Avington toward Dorburn Castle. Brightly colored Avington flags adorned the light poles, and people lined the road to the castle hoping to catch a glimpse of the royal family. Archer sat on Anna's lap happily blowing spit bubbles. Dorian couldn't help chuckling at the contented little boy.

Dorian admired Anna for insisting that Archer come along with the family to public events. When he and Philip were young, they were relegated to the care of one of the many nannies that came and went. At least in some ways, times had changed.

As they drove through the city, Philip and Anna waved and smiled, while Dorian drummed his fingers along the top of the door frame, counting the minutes until they arrived at the castle, and he could get away.

"You just can't help yourself, can you?" Philip asked in a harsh whisper once the horses were past the gates, and they were away from the watchful gazes of the crowds.

Dorian narrowed his gaze at his brother. "What are you talking about?"

Philip rolled his eyes. "The girl. In the crowd. I saw you making eyes at her. Are you trying to get more bad press?"

Dorian's lips curled into a smirk as he recalled the kiss the pretty brunette had blown him. "Are you jealous, brother?"

Anna shot him a look that clearly said, *You're a moron,* then turned back to Archer, her lips pressed into a thin line. Dorian lifted an indifferent shoulder and shifted his gaze back to Philip, who let out a snort.

"I have higher standards than that, *brother*," Philip retorted. "You know as well as I do that the media is watching you like a hawk right now. They aren't going to have missed that exchange."

Dorian grinned. "It's not my fault women find me

irresistible."

"Have fun explaining that to Mother when it's tomorrow's headline."

The grin slipped from Dorian's face. While being part of a royal family had always made them of interest to the press, it seemed that lately he'd become their target. No matter what he did, the paparazzi were there spinning their own version of things. *Or someone else's version.* Whatever version sold the most, regardless of whether it was true or not. Tension climbed Dorian's spine and the muscles in his shoulders tightened.

"Whatever," he snapped at Philip. "You don't know what it's like."

"You're right. I don't," Philip conceded. "But I don't go out of my way to attract negative attention either."

Dorian held his brother's icy glare. "Not all of us were born perfect," he ground out.

Philip's retort was cut off by Anna's motion for silence as the carriages rolled to a stop in front of Dorburn Castle. Dorian shot his brother one last glare before disembarking and joining the rest of the entourage at the entrance to the castle. He stole a quick glance at his watch and released an annoyed sigh. Because the ceremony at the park had run long, he would no longer have time to visit Gatsby before his *required* presence at the state banquet.

Just get through this night and you're done playing Prince for the rest of the summer, he told himself as he pasted a smile on his face and followed the group through the gatehouse and into the great hall. The rest of the group mingled while Dorian stood off to the side and waited. *Three months with no obligations.* He wasn't sure what he was going to do with his time off from royal duties, but he knew it wouldn't be spent in Avington. Anywhere but here. Somewhere far away from his condescending brother and disappointed mother. He began making a mental list of places he'd like to visit when a soft touch on his arm interrupted his thoughts. He turned, and his eyebrows lifted in mild surprise as he met his mother's gaze.

"Is something troubling you, son?" she asked.

Dorian thought he caught a flicker of concern

in her cool blue eyes for just a moment before she glanced around the room, smiling at her guests. His stomach tightened. *Of course, she was concerned. Concerned that he wasn't doing his part.*

"You know I don't like these events, Mother."

Her gaze held his for what seemed like an eternity, the expression on her face unreadable. Dorian refused to look away. He was tired of being forced to take part in all of these formal events where his presence wasn't necessary. Was he acting like a spoiled child? Perhaps, but at this point, he didn't much care. He just wanted the day to be done so he could get on with what he wanted to do, even though he had no idea what that might be.

"I would like to speak with you privately after the banquet," she finally said, her lips curving back into the practiced smile she wore in public.

Dorian stifled a groan but nodded. Satisfied with his response, his mother turned and signaled to the butler that she was ready.

Dorian took his place behind his brother and sister-in-law for the royal procession into the ballroom for the state banquet. He closed his eyes and silently cursed when he saw he'd been paired once again with Ingrid Pelham, Countess of Domhnall. *How had he not seen her earlier? How had she not seen him was the bigger question.* His mother insisted on putting them together at every available opportunity. He was certain it wasn't by chance.

He steeled himself, greeted Ingrid with a forced smile and offered her his elbow, as was his duty. She gripped it like a piranha attacking its prey.

"Dorian," she gushed as she peered up at him through long, dark eyelashes that he was sure were glued onto her eyelids. "I've been looking everywhere for you." She glanced around as though looking to make sure they were alone, then said, "I heard all about your break-up with Candace Easton. You poor thing." She placed her hand on his arm and gave it a light squeeze.

Dorian narrowed his eyes at her honeyed tone, and carefully removed her hand from his arm. *I'm sure you have.* She had made it no secret that she intended to become the next princess of Avington. "Lady Ingrid," he replied curtly and focused his attention forward. He hated to be rude, but he wasn't in the mood to deal with her overt advances.

"Aren't you going to tell me how good I look?" Ingrid turned to the side and batted her eyelashes at him from over her bare shoulder.

Dorian studied her for a moment. She was waif-thin, which was accentuated by the tight-fitting black gown she wore. The black was in stark contrast to her chin-length straight blonde hair. Her wide, cat-like eyes were heavily made up in dark shadow, and sparkly pink makeup accentuated her cheekbones. Dark lipstick lined her heart-shaped lips.

He supposed some men might think she was beautiful. Until she opened her mouth, that is. Just like Candace. Candace was dark to Ingrid's blonde, but wore her makeup in the same dramatic fashion. He wondered if either one of them would be recognizable without it. In his mind, they relied too much on surface glamor and failed to understand that a woman's true beauty came from within.

Dorian forced a smile. "You look lovely, as always."

Ingrid beamed, clearly failing to hear the slight sarcasm in his voice. Thankfully, the line moved, and the procession entered the grand ballroom where the enormous mahogany table had been set for the 150 or so guests who had been invited based upon their cultural or diplomatic links to Avington and Ireland.

Several of the guests, including Ingrid and her family, were regular invitees. Dorian and Ingrid were seated next to one another near the head of the table, and he fought the urge to trade places with the gentleman next to him.

Once all the guests were situated, Queen Sophia stood and welcomed everyone. With her long, dark brown hair swept into a chignon at the nape of her neck and an emerald tiara atop her head, the queen was a stunning woman. Despite his annoyance with her, Dorian admired his mother. She had taken the crown at a young age, after a short illness took the life of her father, King Edward. Dorian had never had the opportunity to meet his grandfather, but he knew he was a well-loved man that ruled his country with wisdom and justice. His mother followed his example and was revered and respected by not only the citizens of Avington, but by leaders of the neighboring European countries as well.

The queen delivered her welcome speech. Dorian listened for a few moments but found his mind wandering once again to possible vacation destinations. He'd already decided to take this trip solo. Maybe he'd spend a little time thinking about what he wanted to do with his life. His mother had been pressuring him a lot more lately to work in an official capacity. He had no desire to ride his brother's coattails and had no interest in being a foreign diplomat.

A round of polite applause brought Dorian out of his reverie, and the guests visited amongst themselves as the staff brought in the meal. Ingrid wasted no time in continuing her flirtation.

"I'm quite put out that you never called." She pursed her painted pink lips together in a pout.

Dorian gritted his teeth. *What was she talking about?* "I don't recall that I was supposed to."

"Well, now that you're single again, there's no reason for us--"

"Us? What are you talking about?" Dorian hissed. He glanced quickly around to see if anyone was listening to them. Everyone appeared to be engaged in their own conversations and he felt a small measure of relief. The last thing he needed, or wanted, was to be romantically linked with her.

"What?" Ingrid widened her eyes in mock innocence and blinked at him. "We're perfect for each other." Her lips curled into a sly smile. "You know, I could help you get over her."

Was she trying to be sympathetic? If so, it wasn't working. Not to mention he didn't think Ingrid possessed a single gram of genuine sympathy for anything that didn't serve some benefit to her. Dorian swallowed hard and forced down his temper.

He had met Candace Easton while he was in the French Riviera with his friends on holiday. She was an American actress that was there on location for a film she was starring in. He'd been captivated by her beauty and charm. They'd quickly become darlings in the media and their relationship was highly publicized.

It hadn't taken very long for Dorian to realize they

had absolutely nothing in common. The entire basis of her attraction to him was his title and what it could do for her acting career. When he'd broken things off just a few short weeks ago, she'd gone ballistic. She began spreading lies about him on every social media outlet she could. Even worse, she partook in countless entertainment television interviews so she could tell *her* side of the story. And her side of the story was nothing close to reality.

That was bad enough, but now Ingrid was trying to use that debacle to position herself closer to him. She wasn't any better than Candace had been. He'd given up on finding someone that would love him for him, and not just because of his title.

Dorian stared at her for a long moment and with a deliberate movement, lifted her hand off his arm. "Ingrid, that's enough," he said, lowering his voice to a barely audible level. "I've warned you before that you and I are not going to happen. You need to stop this nonsense."

She sniffed. "We'll just see about that."

They managed to make it through the rest of the

meal without further incident or comment. After the plates were cleared and the guests dismissed, Dorian headed toward the other end of the castle and approached his mother's study. He couldn't imagine what it was that she wanted to talk to him about, but for some reason he had a feeling that his vacation was about to be taken off the table. He knocked lightly and pushed the door open without waiting for a response.

Dorian stopped short when he saw that Philip occupied one of the two chairs positioned on the other side of the ornate oak desk where his mother sat. Philip glanced at him from over the rim of a teacup and grinned like a cat who'd just swallowed a canary. *Of course, Philip would be involved with whatever grand plan his mother wanted to discuss with him.*

His mother smiled at him as he entered the room. "Dorian, please have a seat." She gestured toward the empty chair next to Philip. Dorian clenched his jaw so hard he thought he might crack a molar, but complied.

"I would like to discuss your royal duties. I feel

as though you've been...floundering a bit since your retirement from the Army," she said.

Duties. Dorian bristled at the word. His whole life was structured around fulfilling his royal duties. He was always surrounded by an entourage of people making sure he followed their carefully orchestrated plans, their itinerary. The few times he'd dared to go off on his own, he'd fallen under the media's unforgiving microscope. He knew he was seen as little more than a disappointment to his mother since his return a year ago from his stint in the Avington Army.

The truth was, Dorian missed being in the military. He liked the structure and sense of purpose it gave him. He'd felt as though he was actually doing something worthwhile while he was enlisted but, as a member of the royal family, he was forced to retire after ten years of service.

Now, he didn't know what to do with his time. It wasn't like he could just go out and get a job. Since the birth of his nephew, and with another niece or nephew on the way, there was little to no chance he'd ever take the throne, not that he wanted to. Philip had been groomed for the crown since the day he was born, and Dorian was happy to let him have the honor, even though his older brother liked to hold it above him on a regular basis.

"I've made arrangements for you to embark on a goodwill tour of the United States," his mother continued. She slid a sheet of paper across her desk toward him. "This is the itinerary. You'll have to meet with security and the press secretary, of course."

Dorian straightened in his chair and his stomach churned as he glanced at the list of appearances he'd be required to make. *Was she serious?* He never made public appearances on behalf of Avington. That duty had always been relegated to Philip. He lifted his gaze to meet hers and his forehead wrinkled.

"You want *me* to go?"

His mother glanced at Philip then back to Dorian. "We thought it might be a good opportunity for you."

We? Dorian's fingers tightened on the arms of the chair. *Of course, his brother had something to do with this plan.* He knew how much Dorian disliked being put on display. Dorian had been looking forward to having some time alone, away, to think. Not to play "prince".

"Why not Philip?" Dorian argued. "He's better at these kinds of things than I am." The words tasted sour coming out of his mouth, but it was true. Philip had a way of making people like him in an instant, no matter where he went. It wasn't like that for Dorian.

"Don't you think it's time you start contributing?" Philip placed his teacup on the desk and stared at Dorian.

A surge of anger shot through Dorian, and he shoved his chair away from the desk. *He didn't need this.*

"That's enough!" His mother slapped her palm on the surface of the desk.

Dorian froze and the two brothers exchanged a guilty glance. Their mother never raised her voice.

She gave them each a pointed glare, then settled her gaze on Dorian and folded her hands on the table. "Quite frankly, Dorian, you need to improve your public image. This will give you an opportunity to do that, as well as boost Avington's relations with the

United States."

Dorian's mouth went dry and his cheeks burned with shame. She was right. He hated that she was right, but she was. "None of what's been said about me is true," he said in a resigned tone.

His mother's mouth tightened. "Nevertheless, it has not been good publicity for Avington. This will give you a chance to show yourself, and Avington, in a positive light."

"If he doesn't screw it up," Philip chortled.

Dorian pressed his lips together. His mother had a point. This would be a good way to improve his reputation. It might not be the vacation he'd had in mind, but maybe this was what he needed. A chance to prove himself. A chance to prove Philip wrong. He sat straighter in the chair and grinned as a lightness filled him. A lightness he'd never felt before.

"Let's do this."

206

About the Author

Laura Ashwood is a USA Today Bestselling author of sweet contemporary romance, historical western romance, and women's fiction.

In her novels, Laura brings to life characters and relationships that will warm your heart and fill you with hope. Her stories often have themes involving redemption, forgiveness, and family.

Laura and her husband live in northeast Minnesota, which is the setting for many of her stories. She has a full time day job as a paralegal, and in her spare time, she likes to read, cook and spend time with her husband. She is a devoted grandmother and chihuahua lover.

She is a member of American Christian Fiction Writers (ACFW) and Faith, Hope & Love Christian Writers (FHLCW).

www.ingramcontent.com/pod-product-compliance
Lightning Source LLC
Chambersburg PA
CBHW021351150726
47989CB00005B/2193